D0443139

Christmas by Accident

Christmas by Accident

CAMRON WRIGHT

SHADOW
MOUNTAIN

Interior illustrations © KALABUKHAVA IRYNA/shutterstock.com

Visit us at shadowmountain.com

Library of Congress Cataloging-in-Publication Data

Names: Wright, Camron Steve, author.
Title: Christmas by accident / Camron Wright.
Description: Salt Lake City, Utah : Shadow Mountain, [2018]
Identifiers: LCCN 2018007099 | ISBN 9781629724768 (hardbound : alk. paper)
Subjects: LCSH: Man-woman relationships—Fiction. | LCGFT: Romance fiction.
 | Christmas fiction.
Classification: LCC PS3623.R53 C45 2018 | DDC 813/.6—dc23
LC record available at https://lccn.loc.gov/2018007099

Printed in the United States of America
Lake Book Manufacturing, Inc., Melrose Park, IL

10 9 8 7 6 5 4 3 2 1

*To those who carry the
Christmas spirit all year long,
and to chocolate!*

Contents

CONTENTS

Chapter 1

Meet Carter Cross

The squeaking of cheap leather shoes scuffing across the room's cut-pile carpet should have forewarned Carter. The footsteps carried the sound of breathing, but Carter didn't move, didn't glance up, didn't twist around.

Instead, he pushed his body against the rubbery rim of his laminate desk and let his restless fingers resume their full frontal attack on his waiting keyboard.

The breathing behind him deepened.

Carter's eyes narrowed, his chin lifted, his gaze leapt word to word as his sentences crawled up the flickering monitor. His story was like Frankenstein's monster rising from the table, and as Carter mouthed each syllable, the paragraph drew a breath. His office chair squeaked.

A distant copy machine gurgled awake. He ran anxious hands through tousled hair as he read:

Asphalt streaked below Ashton Blake and his motorcycle like a swollen spring river rushing beneath a bridge. The lane's painted center lines pulsed past so hypnotically that the man began to count—two, three, four, five. The curved road reminded him of a woman draped in Chinese silk, and he couldn't help but lean his bike close, so close he could have kissed pavement. WHAM—a watermelon-sized boulder suddenly slammed onto the road and clipped the front tire of his Triumph Tiger 800, sending it into a horrific skid.

A nearby clock ticked with apparent glee and appreciation. It was the most exciting thing written in the wearisome office in weeks. Carter's jaw tightened. He studied his last sentence. Should he use the em dash or a comma?

The breathing behind him burst into a scold. "You're embellishing again, aren't you? Even after Harold warned you, *no more embellishing!*"

It was an assault that cracked the silence, punctured the pleasure, let the lingering contentment that had pooled around Carter spill to the floor and drain away. He despised these moments, the first glimmers of recognition after being yanked back to reality. It was dreaming of tanning on a tropical beach, surrounded by bikini-clad beauties, only to be awakened by honking on the street outside his cold apartment—and to roll over to remember that, at age twenty-eight, he was still alone. It was believing that a college education would make an honest difference in the workplace, only to receive a single offer of employment at Business Alliance Deposit Insurance, an establishment so drab and boring it was all that Carter could do to not bludgeon himself to death every morning with his company-issued desktop stapler.

"Well?" the voice behind him pressed. "Why do you embellish?"

The question rolled around in Carter's head, searched for a rational explanation. When Carter didn't answer— didn't move—Lenny, his shorter, balding coworker pressed harder.

"We're insurance adjusters, Carter. Our job is to describe accidents as succinctly as possible." His voice was high, almost scratchy. "We don't embellish! If Harold finds out you've embellished again, he'll . . ." Lenny's words trailed off, as if the punishment would be too horrendous for any human to bear.

Carter's shoulders dropped. His cheeks twitched. He released a long, laden breath before he spun around to face Lenny directly. He wouldn't offer him the satisfaction of anger.

"It's not embellishing, Lenny. It's called creativity." His

tone was almost transparent. "It's describing the accident with words that make the situation clear. That's my job as a claims adjuster. Harold can't get mad at that!"

But the surrender in his reply answered for him. *Yes, Harold undeniably could.*

Lenny pushed sagging glasses against his face, then, with a puff of exasperation, leaned in to peruse Carter's screen. "You haven't always been like this. What happened?" When Carter said nothing, Lenny continued, "I taught you better. You need to follow company policy." He wiped at his nose with a starched handkerchief.

"Otherwise . . ." His head began fish-flopping from side to side, and as he forced out the gruesome truth, he stepped back to create distance.

" . . . Carter, you'll get *fired!*"

Chapter 2

Meet Abby McBride

Abigail McBride—Abby to her friends—tapped her pen a dozen times around the word *bamboozle* until she'd created a peppered halo. The usage of the word was fine, even arguably creative, but there were better choices. It was a matter of style, one of the more difficult concepts she struggled to teach new writers.

"Excuse me, Abby, do you have a book on karate?"

Abby stifled a giggle. The customer asking was Mrs. Lenore Jenkins, a store regular who had to be at least eighty-five.

"We do, but I'll only show you if you promise not to hurt me." It was a bad joke, and as soon as the words scampered out, Abby regretted trying to be funny.

"Why would I hurt you, dear?"

"No, of course you wouldn't!" Abby offered an agreeing smile, set aside the manuscript she was editing, and waved her patron forward.

"Fire up that walker and follow me," Abby declared. "The martial arts section is over here."

Mrs. Jenkins had not yet discovered the convenience of ordering books on Amazon—and for that she deserved to be worshiped.

The ReadMore Café was a family business, an eclectic favorite of the locals in Springfield that sat near the eastern bank of the Connecticut River, a place many described as charming. It was half bookstore, half dessert shop, a fact that helped ensure ReadMore's survival. When the big bookstore chains rolled into town in the late '90s, followed by burgeoning online sales that extinguished many of the country's independent bookstores, the ReadMore Café flourished. While it was true that ReadMore's customers could buy books online for less, Abby's uncle, company owner Mannie McBride, had devised a secret weapon: Apple Crostata Streusel. And that was not all. The place served an array of gourmet pastries, pies, puddings, and pleasures that many claimed would bring world peace. Even their sandwiches were, as a columnist for the local paper had once noted, *rapturous.*

The bookstore/café was located in a quaint, century-old building that was once the city library. While rich with charm, it also meant that on occasion the staff had to explain to a few of Mrs. Jenkins's contemporaries that *no,* books couldn't be checked out, they had to be purchased.

Today, after Abby made certain that both Mrs. Jenkins and her walker were under control, she headed over to the café area of the store to help wipe tables.

In addition to Mannie and Abby, the business employed a half dozen book and food lovers of assorted sizes, ages, and tastes. One of the mainstays was Rosabelle (Rosa) Reinoso, a middle-aged, silver-haired woman of German descent, as plump as she was spunky. She'd been with the store since the heyday of *Sophie's Choice,* a book that still rested on her nightstand table. Even more impressive, a few years ago she had inherited a respectable amount of money—enough to retire—and yet she stayed.

Abby suspected it was the irresistible desserts created by ReadMore's master chef, André Boisen—and she was likely right. As she approached Rosa, she watched the woman's lips pinch into a heart. Her fingers wrapped a cup that whiffed of nutmeg, vanilla, and cinnamon—a new eggnog creation that André had been testing in the kitchen.

"It's *egglessnog*!" Rosa beamed, her words slurring as her tongue licked across her lip.

"I beg your pardon?" Abby replied.

"He made his eggnog recipe without using any eggs, just to see if he could do it!" She was bouncing—*all* of Rosa was bouncing. "I love him, just LOVE HIM!" Rosa declared with all the passion of a love-struck teenager. She pressed the mug toward Abby's chin, let the willing vapors rush at her nose, brush her cheek, caress her neck, and tease the auburn hair that draped amply across her shoulders. Abby took the mug, sipped, sighed, and then eagerly licked cinnamon-laced cream from the rim with her tongue. For a moment, she had the urge to wrap in a warm blanket.

"I love him too!" she declared. "We'd better not tell his wife!"

André and his wife, Ziva, had come to the ReadMore Café a few years earlier to run the café side of the business. André's uncle had worked for Mannie in the past and offered his highest recommendation. The young couple had been trained in Denmark, and, as Mannie put it, "They blend chocolate, butter, and cream together so sensuously, I have to leave the room."

As Abby took another satisfying sip of André's culinary handiwork, her gaze circled from the mug to the back room, to the cash register up front, and then back to the mug. The sweet smell of the eggnog started wheels churning in Abby's head.

"It's too early," Rosa declared before Abby had uttered a word.

"Too early for what?" she pretended.

"Child, don't you dare play coy with me. It's dripping like rain from your guilty face. You're going to put out the Christmas books!"

Abby briefly considered lying, but instead she attempted an appeal to reason. "Have you not looked outside? It's been getting colder! Leaves are falling! It's going to storm. It's that time of year. Why not put out the Christmas books?"

Rosa's stubby fingers were already spread out for counting. "One, it's not yet Halloween. Two, it's not yet Thanksgiving. Three . . ."

It had been a rhetorical question, and Abby was no longer listening. She almost skipped toward the empty book cart in the back of the store. It didn't take her long to gather a sizable assortment of holiday books, wheel them up to a table beside the register up front, and stack them into the shape of a Christmas tree.

She was looking for ribbon to craft a star for the top when her cell phone rang.

"Hi, this is Abby." She listened, pushing the phone

tight against her ear. "I'm sorry, you faded out. Can you say that again?" The news furrowed her brow. Her body stiffened. "Yes, Mannie is my uncle." A longer pause followed. She reached for the table to steady herself. "I see. I'll be right there!"

Rosa shuffled toward her from across the room. Abby's eye muscles tensed. Her lips quivered. Her knees nearly buckled. She pulled the phone away from her ear, but her grip was like iron. Before Rosa could reach her, Abby jammed the phone into her pocket and lurched toward the front door.

"I have to go," she called back. Her words were shaking. "Rosa, can you close?" She didn't wait for an answer.

"Certainly! Abby, dear, what's wrong?"

Tears were leaking now from Abby's eyes. The words scarcely choked out. "It's Mannie! Something's terribly wrong! He's been taken to the hospital!"

Chapter 3

The Girl's Picture

The rain was turning into sleet as Carter arrived at Nemo Sushi, a new restaurant that had opened near his apartment. A blonde hostess, slight of build and wearing an orange-and-white-striped hat, pulled open the door. Her badge read *Where fish are food (not friends).* She had arctic-blue eyes and a princess chin. Her stare lifted to meet Carter's, and then lingered longer than company policy might suggest.

"Hi, there! Welcome," she greeted, looking as alluring as a woman is able when wearing orange and white stripes.

Short of a nod, Carter didn't seem to notice. His fingers were clenched, his shoulders were hunched, his stride was hurried. He spied Yin already seated in a booth and scurried in across from him.

"You made it," Yin said.

"Despite the rain!" Carter replied.

Yin Shyu had been Carter's roommate and best friend for nearly four years. He was in the United States on a student visa that let him stay as long as he was enrolled in school. It meant that Yin had a degree in mathematics, one in biology, and was currently eleven credits shy in computer science. Although Yin had a slight Asian accent, he spoke English better than most Americans.

"You okay?" Yin asked. "You seem angry."

"My mother called," Carter confirmed. "She left a message."

"How's she doing? What did she say?"

"I've told you about my parents, correct?" Exasperation wormed into his words.

"I don't know. What about them?" Yin asked.

"My dad's a trial attorney in Washington State; he's the kind who despises losing."

"Yeah?"

"So a few years ago, my mom got tired of the pressure and filed for a change of venue."

"A what?"

"It means they split up. Yin, my parents are divorced."

"Sure, I know. You've told me. We talked about it."

Carter leaned forward. "But here's the thing: I knew that after spending some time apart, they would eventually get back together. Children have a way of sensing those things. Otherwise, their world would shatter, right?" His eyes pleaded for agreement.

Yin shrugged.

"Anyway, Mom said she wants me to come home for Christmas. I haven't been back for the last two."

"That sounds great. I think you should go. Christmas is about family."

A trickle of sweat snaked its way down Carter's back. When he continued, his voice was lumpy. "She wants me to come back this Christmas because . . . she's met someone new. Yin, my mother is getting remarried."

❄

The weary hospital nurse hadn't told Abby what was wrong, just that her uncle had been admitted and it was requested that she come as soon as possible. As she now drove alone through freezing rain and crushing gloom, imagination schemed with anxiety.

"You can't leave me, Mannie!" Abby cried to no one. "You're the only family I've got!"

She was right. Mannie had raised her since she was three, when her parents had been taken in a tragic camping accident. A malfunctioning heater had filled the room of their cabin with carbon monoxide as they slept—and they never woke up. Thankfully, little Abby had insisted on sleeping in the adjacent room with the drafty window so she could make faces at the moon, like her mother had taught her, and then watch for it to wink back. A mother's simple game had saved a little girl's life.

Mannie was six years older than his brother, had never married, and, as a man who traveled at whim, was in no condition to raise a child—but who is? The thought of sending his tiny niece to a distant relative—or worse, foster care—was out of the question. And so, for slightly more than two decades, Mannie had been the only father Abby could remember.

She reached now to turn up the wipers before finding they were already flapping across the glass at full speed. Between beats, sleety pebbles smacked against the window, insisting they be let in. Her car was a Ford Fiesta, but at the moment it offered no reason to party.

On a good day—any other day—the drive from Springfield to the hospital in Northampton would take just a half hour. Tonight, a backed-up freeway had forced Abby onto alternate routes, unfamiliar roads. The GPS on her phone kept losing its signal and Abby was losing her composure.

"What could be wrong with him?" Her words stumbled forward and fell out, but there was no one there to catch them. "He's seemed tired lately, taking more days off than usual. I should have known. I should have asked. I should have done something!"

Playing with *should haves* in the dark was a dangerous game.

The road ahead turned, but when Abby touched the brake, nothing happened. She tapped repeatedly. The car ignored her. Her hands clutched at the wheel. She turned right. Nothing. Left. Still nothing.

Unbeknownst to Abby, as the temperature had dropped, the movement of the molecules in the fallen rain had slowed, causing the oxygen atoms to snuggle into orderly crystalline shapes—meaning that water pooling against the road's surface on the upcoming curve was now a treacherous sheet of ice.

The car began to pirouette precipitously to the left. As it spun, its headlights strobed across a grouping of trees waiting at the road's edge—two, three, four—and then the flickering light slipped over the bank and fell into darkness.

Abby sucked in a breath, tried to release, but her lungs refused to let go. A ripple of air wafted across her face—or was it fear?—as the muscles in her body constricted. Her cramping fingers clenched so tightly, the leather wheel could also no longer breathe.

In the dark, Abby screamed.

❄

The sun was up, though barely, as Carter pushed open the gate at the insurance company's tow lot. It was triage for cars, a holding yard where the most heavily damaged vehicles were assessed. Carter preferred to come early not simply because there were fewer people, but because the light was softer. It made for better pictures.

Carter had a slew of accident reports on his docket, so he shuffled through his paperwork to find the first: a white Jeep Grand Cherokee. It was the only Grand Cherokee on the lot, so it was easy to locate. It was hit in the front, on the driver's side. According to the report, the accident had been caused by an uninsured driver who ran a red light.

Carter stooped beside the car, bent to the ground

to survey the undercarriage. It took only a moment to list the needed repairs: new side panel, undercarriage protector, and suspension. They'd have to pull the engine to check for damage to the camshaft fastener and the connecting rod, but that would certainly be doable. He'd itemize everything back at the office, enter it all into the computer, but he could tell already this vehicle was not even close to a total loss. Yes, it would require several thousand dollars' worth of repairs and be in the shop at least a full week, but this car would absolutely be back on the road again.

With his notes complete, Carter snatched the company camera, a digital SLR, from his bag. He worked like a robot, snapping a picture from the front—*click,* the rear—*click,* and then each side—*click, click.*

Next up was a gray Hyundai Elantra. It had rear-ended a pickup truck on the freeway. The routine was the same. Assess the damage. List what needed to be repaired and what needed to be replaced. Take pictures to document accordingly, and then move on to the next vehicle.

The cars blurred. Reports were compiled. Notes were scribbled. *Click, click, click.* Next. Another, then another, and then another still.

Last up was a Ford Fiesta, red. This one, sadly, didn't fare as well as the others. It appeared to have hit a tree or two—perhaps a power pole, because there was massive damage that raked both the front and side. Carter had handled enough accidents to know this car was spinning—rather violently, he guessed—prior to impact. He line-itemed the destruction: airbag deployed, mutilated side panels, three windows shattered with the glass gone, displaced front end, bent frame, and a broken axle. While Carter would tally the damage later, he already knew one thing for certain: this car was headed to the scrapyard.

He snapped the customary pictures—*click, click, click, click*—closed his file, and then glanced around. He was still alone in the yard.

His eyelids lifted. His lips followed. It was as if he were seeing today's surroundings for the first time. Morning sunbeams dipped around the curve of a chrome fender, danced across the beam of a pickup's tailgate, and then ricocheted in all directions through the prism of a smashed windshield. He may have even heard them snicker as they flittered away.

Carter pulled the camera to his eye, leaned in close to the Fiesta, bent low, and framed the mangled metal of the manifold. *Click.*

Next, he slid around to the front, nodded knowingly

to the grill, then cropped ever so tightly as the metal melted into coffers of chrome. *Click. Click.*

Ripples in the roof became corrugated steel crags. Swells in the crimson hood morphed into dunes of Martian sand.

An artist was at work.

Carter was loose and relaxed, soaking in the sun so deeply it was leaving puddles. He kept circling his unwitting metal subject. *Click. Click. Click.*

He pried open the driver's door wide enough to climb inside. It was a photographer's wonderland: *Click,* the peppered grain of a leather-wrapped steering wheel. *Click,* a shot of fragmented glass that could be ice crystals. *Click,* a curve in the plump leather seat that was almost voluptuous.

And then, as he hunched over trying to focus on rumpled floor mats, he spied the corner of a photo pinched between the seat and the center console. He extracted it with two fingers slowly, carefully, like a new father handling his child's first soiled diaper.

Personal items were usually retrieved before the insurance company tabulated damage. If adjusters did find personal articles left behind, protocol required that they note them in the salvage yard log, lock them in a designated bin, and then notify the involved parties so they could arrange for pickup.

Carter held the photo to the light. It was a picture of a woman—orphan eyes, slender nose, mid-twenties, wearing a soft floral blouse that must have been selected to complement her coordinating smile. There was a name written on the back: Abby McBride. Carter squinted as he tried to recall if that was the name of the insured. It didn't sound familiar, but his assigned accidents were sorted by vehicle make and model, not by driver name. It was akin to a doctor who couldn't place the face of a patient whose life he had saved but would long remember the threatening wound or medical condition.

Several seconds passed as Carter stared at the girl, the girl staring back, until the sound of an opening gate startled him. Lenny was arriving.

"Hi, Carter. Have you been here long?" Lenny asked as Carter climbed out of the car.

"Just finishing up." Perfect timing.

Carter collected his gear, ducked into his own car, and then drove from the lot toward the office. Two blocks away, while waiting for a traffic light to change, he pulled out the picture from among his papers and gave it another protracted glare. It carried a puzzling question that was now crinkling his forehead and causing him to lean forward in his seat. The girl in the picture, Abby McBride, was likely the person who had been driving the totaled car.

Was she injured? Did she survive?

Chapter 4

Meet Mannie McBride

Mannie McBride edged forward on the mattress and then back. Trying to get comfortable in a hospital bed was like lounging on LEGOs. He was a large man with a determined frame, whose arms, chest, and head sprouted curls of gray hair. For a man who was recently rushed unconscious to the hospital, he appeared to be abundantly energetic. More important, as his niece who sat next to him had twice pointed out, the man donned a hospital gown with confidence, like an attorney attired in Armani.

Fitting the image, Mannie was grilling his niece like she was a defendant on trial.

"Headaches?" he asked.

"No," Abby reassured.

"Back pain?" he wondered.

"None."

"Bruises?"

She glanced up from her chair. Her head wobbled. "Actually, I am having a sharp pain I just can't seem to get rid of—right here." She pointed with concern to her posterior. "It's a pain in my butt that is getting worse the longer you go on, so watch my lips and listen. I told you, Mannie, besides the slight bump to my head and a few scratches, I'm fine—though my Fiesta isn't feeling so festive."

"Any word from the insurance company?" he asked, relenting.

"They assured me an adjuster would be assigned and someone would contact me shortly."

A distinguished-looking man in a white coat stepped into the room to interrupt. He was either the doctor or a lost cruise ship waiter.

Mannie spoke up quickly. "Abby, this decent man is here to check my blood pressure. While he does, do me a favor. Run to the lobby and grab me a pack of those mints I love."

Her eyes curled. "Which mints are those?"

"I don't remember what they're called. The whitish ones that say *mints* on the package."

She studied him warily, hesitated for a moment, and

then scooted out the door. When Mannie was certain she was gone, his lips feigned a grin. It was an errand that would buy him fifteen minutes with the man who had, in fact, come to deliver his prognosis.

Mannie turned now toward the doctor, who was waiting to make eye contact. The news couldn't be good because the white-coated man was holding his clipboard like a shield. Perhaps he'd had a disastrous prior experience.

"Mannie, we've run some tests," he finally said, "and we've confirmed that you have amyloidosis."

"Amy-la-who?"

The doctor sat on the bed bedside Mannie, so he was either very tired or the news had to be *very* bad. The weary, white-coated man continued, "It's a rare disease in which proteins are abnormally deposited in your body, not broken down correctly. They have accumulated in your heart, causing a thickening of the muscle walls. In your case . . ." his mouth puckered as if the words were suddenly bitter, "you have a type called *light chain,* and unfortunately it's the most difficult to treat."

Mannie was lagging a sentence behind. "My heart?" he asked.

"More than your heart. It's rapidly clogging your liver, kidneys, and nervous system."

Mannie's chin lowered, but not because he was

24

surprised. It was his body, after all, and since the fainting spells, the arm pain, and the dizziness—all of which had begun months ago—it suddenly made sense: a battle had been raging in his chest. The doctor confirmed it: battalions of his own cells were already in full retreat. *Amy-whatever* had flanked the line and was pillaging his organs like a Viking army. What Mannie didn't know was the timing of the final defeat.

"Is there anything I can do?" he asked.

The doctor bowed, almost in prayer. His voice turned timid. "A transplant is the only option, but unfortunately . . ."

Unfortunately was a sad word, Mannie thought. "What is it?"

"With your other organs already affected, you won't be a suitable candidate to receive a heart. Honestly, even if you were, I'm not sure your other organs would survive a transplant. There's a chance, but it's very slim."

The next question was already waiting. "How long do I have, Doctor?"

The doctor stood. "Your heart is acutely enlarged, and based on my past experience—"

Mannie was getting impatient. "How long?"

"I'm sorry to tell you, Mr. McBride, but in truth, you'll be lucky if you make it to Christmas."

Chapter 5

Addendum A

Business Alliance Deposit Insurance: the company name alone would put most people into a trance, which meant it was industry perfect—save for one minor issue. In the late '90s, when acronyms were popular, the company's rebranding rollout lasted only days until someone pointed out they were advertising B.A.D. Insurance. No heads rolled, but the CEO took an early retirement, and the naming mishap was still being laughed at in business school case studies countrywide.

The accident reports that Carter now typed—one after another, and *without* embellishment—were so straightforward and boring even the screen flickered like it might doze off. When Carter got to the Ford Fiesta, he had already filled in the case number, time, place, location, and contact information before he realized it was the car in which he had found the photo of the girl.

His neck pivoted as he examined the room. With no one watching, he slid open the drawer of his desk and took another glance at the girl's picture, the photo he should have reported finding in her car. He knew by now she had survived. He'd checked the notes from her initial call to dispatch, which had confirmed that despite the damage to her car, she had escaped with no significant injuries.

Carter scratched at his chin. In the myriad of reports he'd entered over the years, he'd seldom had the opportunity to place a face with an accident. Perhaps that was why he'd kept her photo.

He tabbed to the description field, watched the curious cursor blink back as it prodded him. He placed the girl's picture closer. *This is Miss McBride's accident,* he thought. *It seems only fitting she have a good view.*

His fingertips touched the keys, then waited for direction.

One more look around the office. One more glimpse at the girl's upturned lips.

If there were any hesitation as to what he would do next, it was squashed by the blandness of the surrounding room. The drab grey walls were so lifeless, they needed CPR. The carpet so hideous, it would scare a crack house. The cubicle fabric so neutral, Switzerland may move in and pick out furniture. Even the mandated music droning on in the background could cause the bravest of elevators to plunge to its own death.

How could they not comprehend that the weight of this place was crushing him? How could they not understand he was drowning?

Carter remembered his mother, her upcoming marriage to a stranger. It was a thought that was dashed to the floor by memories of his breakup with Darcy, his now ex-girlfriend. He'd read that disasters come in threes. What was next? An earthquake?

His fingers twitched. One last time his head commanded them to simply type in the mindless accident report as succinctly as possible and move on. His heart nudged otherwise. He turned to the photo sitting on his desk. "So, Abby," he whispered, "tell me about your accident."

She didn't move, didn't blink.

"What was that icy road like?" he asked.

He waited, as if the picture would answer, and it must have, because he began to tap at the keys.

Abby tensed, shuddered, and then shrieked. Lightning

ripped the sodden, sleeting clouds like they were pieces of two-dollar fabric. The icy sheet crackled beneath the load of the helpless tires on the terrified girl's car.

Carter's chin lifted. His shoulders broadened. He inhaled an encouraging breath.

The car was sliding, shaking, sliding, as she gripped frantically at the steering wheel like a drunk grappling for his last drink—but it was too late.

He cracked his knuckles, flexed his fingers, rested them comfortably again on the anxious keyboard.

Through the black night she could make out the cliff's edge, and in a remorseful second, she realized that all that separated her from an agonizing death was a small grouping of trees.

Carter edged closer to his screen. His eyes were barely slits. He could no longer hear the incessant background music. He had forgotten the fabric that draped his cubical, ignored the ugly carpet spread beneath his shoes, overlooked his lifeless office walls.

Carter was writing.

Beep!

An error box opened. It told Carter that the description field had reached its character limit. To continue, he had to tab his cursor to *Addendum A.*

29

He tabbed. He continued.

"So this is how it ends," Abby thought as time slowed, as she felt the throb of each heartbeat, as each moment propelled her closer and closer to the cliff's edge. In the remaining seconds, her storied life flashed before her eyes, and then, just before impact, as if she instantly understood that everything would be okay in the end—Abby smiled.

"Carter!"

Carter's fingers quit typing. It wasn't the voice of Lenny calling from over his shoulder, a notion that, for the first time ever, brought sadness.

"You've got exactly fifteen seconds to get into my office to explain *what on earth you're doing!*"

The gray-suited man wearing the tie that didn't match, the man with flushed cheeks and thrashing hands, the man who was currently squawking furiously at Carter, was Harold Rotterdamm.

Mr. Rotterdamm was Carter's boss.

❄

The veins in Harold's neck pulsed like a Def Leppard migraine. Beads of sweat crawled out of his hairline. Had it been ancient Rome and Harold's office

the Colosseum, Carter would already be missing an arm
. . . or worse.

Carter waited in a chair while Harold brought up
the offending file on his computer. The man clenched his
computer's mouse so forcefully, Carter thought he heard
it squeal.

Harold opened the file, dragged the cursor to the description field, and highlighted the text so the men could
read it together.

"I don't know if you think you're Mark Twain, or
Stephen King, or . . ." Harold froze. His mouth was round,
but no sound rolled out. It was obvious that his brain
was searching desperately for another famous author—
anyone—but he was drawing a blank. Apparently, Harold
wasn't much of a reader.

Carter didn't keep him hanging. "No, I don't."

He could try to explain why he'd been so . . . *descriptive,* but he wasn't sure he could articulate the reasons himself. Besides, what would be the point? He was
talking to a man who didn't just love his job, his idea of
an office party was to sort paper clips and link spread-
sheets. Instead, Carter twisted the truth.

"Harold, I'm writing the accident descriptions with
a little more flair for the benefit of those who read them
later, to keep their interest. Is that so bad?"

Harold's shoulders spun sideways as he wound up. His confident smirk announced that he could hit this one out of the park blind. "Read them later?" His eyes almost popped. "I've told you! *Nobody is ever going to read them later!*"

Harold coiled and swung again. "Carter, you used Addendum A! *Nobody in the company's history has ever used Addendum A!*"

Carter wondered why it was there, considered asking, but thought the better of it.

"And another thing," Harold added, raising a finger to match his voice. "You wrote that right before impact she smiled. *Smiled?* Why on earth would she smile?" His stare was a sword. He raised it, pointed, and then plunged for Carter's heart. "*That is just terrible writing!*"

Carter bent forward in his chair. The muscles in his neck flexed. His head tipped. Call him frustrated, complain he was overly dramatic, insist he was out of line, and yell at him for writing descriptions that were too long and even pointless, but was it really necessary to get personal?

"Look," he declared, staring down Harold for the first time. "The writing is a bit . . . melodramatic, for sure, but . . ."

Carter was ready to defend his honor to the death,

if necessary, when Harold clicked to the *Policy Status Page*. A solid red bar blinked at the top of the screen, as if pleased to interrupt.

Harold stopped. He pivoted in his chair to face the screen. His eyes, already narrow, scrunched tighter. Carter's eyes followed. Confusion had waltzed in, taken both men by the hands, and asked them to dance. Neither could say why the message hadn't been noticed before now. It would have negated so much drama.

Claim denied. Auto policy lapsed forty-five days prior to the accident.

Harold coughed. He straightened. He looked to Carter for answers. "Her policy lapsed? Why weren't you alerted when you first entered the claim?" His mouth remained open—gaping. The only sound was the air snorting in and out of Harold's nose.

Carter listened, puzzled, pondered. After moments turned to seconds, his lips also parted. "It could be a glitch. I . . . I'm not certain."

"We need to inform the claimant right away, before this goes any further." Harold scanned for the address. "Look, she is here in town. I'll print a *Denial of Claim* letter and have Lenny drop it off this afternoon."

"Lenny? No, I'll take it," Carter volunteered.

Harold turned. Their gazes locked. "That won't be necessary, Carter."

"Why not?"

"Because you're fired."

Chapter 6

The Big Idea

Abby fought to stay focused. She edited book manuscripts on the side and had told her client that she'd have his story done by midweek. However, when she inadvertently doodled a frowny clown in the margin, she understood it was time to pack up her things and tend to more pressing matters.

"Seven? Can you and Rosa cover for me? I'm going home to make sure everything is ready for Mannie."

While Rosa was ReadMore's most tenured employee, Seven was the store's newest, and the one with the most unusual name. Despite the incessant questions—*Is Seven a nickname? Why did your parents give you a number instead of a name? Do you have siblings named One through Six?*—she seemed to adore the attention.

As for the name, the truth was rather simple: she was born on the seventh of July, at seven in the morning, in room seven, at the hospital on Seventh Street, in addition to several other coincidences that even she admitted got a little convoluted.

She was rake skinny, with bleached hair, tipped red, donning seven back braids, each threaded with seven multihued beads. Despite the focus, she wasn't hired because of her appearance or her name. She was a top-of-her-class student at Western New England studying Biomedical Engineering—and she loved to read.

"Not a problem!" Seven replied. "How's Mannie doing, anyway? Anything new to report?"

Abby fussed as she gathered papers into her purse. "He's scheduled to come home tomorrow. Fingers remain crossed." But she was speaking to the floor.

"You seem hesitant," Seven said, reaching for Abby's arm.

When Rosa heard them discussing Mannie, she bounded over to join the huddle.

Abby assembled her words. "I'm only concerned because I don't feel like I've heard a reasonable answer as to why he fainted, why his arms felt numb. Mannie says it's low blood sugar, but how can anyone who works here . . ." Abby pointed across the room to André's desserts, " . . . have low blood sugar?"

"Did you talk with the doctors?" Seven asked.

"They wouldn't say anything. They told me I had to speak with Mannie."

Rosa's glossy eyes widened. "Yes, it's because of the hippie laws!"

Seven chuckled. "I believe you mean HIPAA."

Rosa's head couldn't nod any faster. "Yes, yes, exactly. Doctors won't tell you anything these days!"

"But Mannie is feeling better, right?" Seven confirmed.

"Yes, he seems to be," Abby answered.

Rosa's head was still bobbing. "Please give him our love, dear. Tell him he's missed. We all wish we could give him a big hug." The words rolled out with unbridled enthusiasm, as if she were auditioning for the role of a garish German grandmother. All that was missing was a pinch of the man's cheek. "And take him a dessert," she added, hurrying to the café's expansive glass case to pick one out herself.

Abby and Seven exchanged glances. Seven gave Abby one last squeeze on her arm. "He'll be fine, Abby," Seven assured. "He'll be fine."

*

Harold gave Carter a box when a bag would have been sufficient. As he silently gathered his things, Lenny loitered in the background. As on any other day, Carter did his best to ignore him.

There wasn't much to take—his Simpsons mouse pad, a Chick-fil-A calendar featuring monthly discounts, his favorite coffee mug engraved with the words *My Life Is Loosely Based on a True Story.*

Why hadn't he nested here? he wondered. It was true he didn't care for the job—that much was obvious to any idiot—but why? Was it the environment, or was it him? Would he ever find his purpose in life, his passion?

Lenny stepped from behind—always from behind. "You know Harold is giving me all of your cases, right? At least until they hire someone else to replace you."

Carter locked and loaded. He whipped around ready to tell Lenny how deep he could shove his whiny complaints, but then he noticed the man's pink, puffy eyes, his splotchy, fearful face. Lenny looked as if he might spontaneously burst into tears.

Carter's arms dropped. His fingers rolled open. His muscles exhaled. "Are you okay?" he finally asked.

Lenny's voice was low, brittle, confused. "You don't seem sad," he said quizzically.

At least the man was observant. Carter motioned for Lenny to take a seat, then sat down beside him. "I've never been fired," Carter confided. "I guess I'm not sure what it's supposed to feel like."

The words must have been heavy because as Carter spit them out, his shoulders lifted. He'd never discussed his feelings with Lenny, which made it ironic to be doing so now, considering it was Carter's last day on the job—yet he found their talk strangely satisfying.

"I suppose I should be angry," Carter continued, "and I guess I am, but part of me wants to climb onto my desk and Snoopy dance. Is that bad?"

Lenny glanced around. "I probably wouldn't do that."

"On one hand," Carter added, "I'm excited to find another job, something I'll enjoy." For Carter, relief was flowing into the room like a fire hose. "But on the other hand, I'm worried that such a thing doesn't exist."

"Are you fine for money?" Lenny wondered.

"Money?" It was the first time he'd considered it, now that his paycheck had been cut off. He tallied a quick counting of finances in his head. He had a $1,000 emergency fund—*thank you, Dave Ramsey*—and enough in his savings to last a few months, if he was careful. Surely he could find another job soon. "I'll be okay, Lenny. Thanks for asking."

"I suppose I should tell you . . . well, never mind. It doesn't matter now." Lenny's shoulders deflated.

"What is it?"

"I put your name in to work with me on this year's Christmas party—even though I know you've said you hate Christmas. Otherwise, Eleanor will do it and she wants to play Christmas Sing-Along Surprise again and so I thought if you and me . . . well, forget it, 'cause it won't be happening."

"That's . . ." Carter's brain played word search. " . . . I guess *terrible.* I detest that game as well."

"If there is anything you need . . . or, you know, if you still want to go to lunch sometime, please let me know."

Carter swallowed, pulled a tissue from the box on his desk, and handed it across to Lenny just in case.

The silence didn't seem to bother Lenny. "It dawns on me, Carter," Lenny added, "that we've never honestly talked like this, heart to heart. Then you get fired, and now . . . it almost feels like we're . . . I guess friends. Do you think we're like the married couples who fight and fight and fight up until they get divorced, and only then do they become close?"

Carter backstepped. His face blanched. A man had to have his limits. "Lenny!" he demanded. "Please never repeat that again!"

Still, as a token of the unexpected bonding, Carter opened his drawer to retrieve his favorite pen, a parting gift that he would leave with Lenny. When the drawer slipped open, beaming up at him from inside was the catalyst for the day's absurdity, the picture of Abby McBride. A gnawing notion shadowed the girl's grin.

Carter rocked forward. A plan was taking shape. "Lenny, do you have that *Denial of Claim* letter yet from Harold?"

"Yes, it's on my desk. I told him I'd drop it off this afternoon."

Carter let the thought stew and boil, stirring it slightly. "Hey, listen . . . I'm thinking that on my way out the door, I should clean up my own mess. Why don't you let *me* drop it off?"

Lenny stood beside Carter, shifted his weight. "I don't know, Carter. That's against company policy, and Harold said—"

"I'm merely trying to help. Besides, I'm being paid

through the end of the day, so technically I'm an employee until five o'clock."

Even Lenny couldn't argue with the logic. "That's true! I guess it would be all right, but make sure she gets it!"

Carter handed his pen to Lenny, followed the man to his desk. "You can count on it!"

❄

Chimes sounded at the ReadMore as Carter pushed through the door. It was an old-fashioned, mechanical contraption where a springy bar attached to a solid brass bell that jingled like a caffeinated elf every time the door swung open.

Carter stepped inside and scanned for Abby McBride. The place was bustling with customers.

"Hi, may I help you?"

Carter turned to the voice—she wasn't the girl in the photo, but as he read her name tag, his forehead creased. She must have noticed him squinting because her subsequent laugh was plentiful and genuine.

"Yes," she said to a question he hadn't yet raised. "Seven is my real name."

"No, I . . ." Carter smothered a smile. "It's a great

name, truthfully. I'm looking for Abby McBride. This is the address I was given. Does she work here?"

"I'm sorry, she had to go home early. May I leave her a message?"

Carter grasped a manila folder that contained both the letter and Abby's photo. He reached in, let his fingertips brush them both, but extracted only the sealed envelope. He passed it to the numbered clerk. "Please make sure she gets this."

Seven offered a slight bow. "I'll put it in a safe place for her."

As Seven headed toward the register, Carter pivoted to leave, but between him and the door was a towering, tree-shaped display of books—Christmas books.

While it was true he had just been fired and may have been overly cynical at the moment, he couldn't stop his head from physically shaking. "Christmas?" he grumbled to no one. "Never mind it's still October!"

The display, while eye-catching, reminded Carter of a party loudmouth, the *let's-talk-about-me* type wearing a flashy suit and a false smile—but Carter wouldn't be intimidated. He reached out and plucked a book at random: *The Christmas Angel.* It couldn't be more than a hundred pages. He cracked the cover and skimmed the first few paragraphs.

His mumbling didn't stop. "Rubbish writing, simply rubbish."

The display, the writing itself, the fact that it was still October, all epitomized Carter's distaste for the holiday. He could wrap it up with a single word and a ribbon: greed.

Pure. Simple. Greed.

He picked up another. *The Christmas Wish*. Also short, also juvenile.

"It's a holiday scam," he said to himself, this time louder. "Hey, here's an idea. How about *The Christmas Con?*"

He picked up yet another. *The Christmas Donkey*. Was there no shame? And more. *The Christmas Stocking, The Christmas Locket, The Christmas Sleigh, The Christmas Town, The Christmas Bear*. As Carter pulled each from the pile, one Christmas truth was clubbing him over the head: "Everyone at Christmas is making a killing except for me!"

The words crossed his tongue, circled twice around his neck, and then plummeted into his opposite ear. The thought planted itself like a seed in his brain, and who could dispute it? The tree-shaped pile with its silly star made of ribbon flaunted the evidence: publishers, retail stores, and writers all were raking in Christmas cash.

His fingers reached out a final time. He plucked an-other book from the stack like he was picking fruit. *The Christmas Candy.* He flipped it open to the first page. As his lips licked the words, the corners of his mouth turned up. Each syllable wrapped in realization.

The seeds had already sprouted, leafed, and were now flowering. "I could write this crap," he said. Although he needed no further convincing, he repeated it again with swelling conviction. "Yes, I could absolutely write this crap!"

"Hi, do you still need help?"

Carter turned. Seven was back.

"Actually, I do have a question." Carter's breathing had quickened. "Tell me about these Christmas books. Do you sell many?"

Seven didn't hesitate. "Christmas books? Sure, as the holiday gets closer they sell like crazy."

Enthusiasm was pulsing now in Carter's veins. He didn't mean to sound obstinate. He just needed to be certain. "Really? Even though most are short, sappy, and printed with big type?"

Seven smiled. "None of that matters at Christmas!"

We have a winner! Carter would have reached out and kissed the girl, had he not expected he'd get slapped or arrested.

He was looking for purpose; he was craving direction. And now, fate had found him, sooner than he'd ever expected. It was time to wrap his arm around opportunity and march together to the land of prosperity.

"I need a Christmas book," Carter announced. It was a developing plan, so even he looked a little surprised at his words.

"Certainly," Seven said. "Which one can I wrap up for you?"

Fireworks were going off in Carter's head. Seven waited. Carter stared back at the pile with determination.

It was a sign, right? He had been fired that very morning for his creative writing, only to stumble across this brilliant idea a few hours later. It was fate. It was destiny. It had to be.

He turned to Seven—such a beautiful name—and, in his excitement, he grabbed her by the shoulders.

"I want one of each!"

"One of each Christmas title?" she confirmed.

He was bouncing now on his toes.

"Yes! I want them all!"

Chapter 7

The Letter

Seven was shelving books when Abby arrived.

"You look frazzled," Seven announced. "Did you take the bus?"

Abby wrestled her unruly hair until it was suitably tied back. When it finally quit trying to squirm free, she perched on a stool beside Seven to catch her breath and stretch her fingers. "Worse. I'm driving Mannie's car until I get mine back, and it's a stick shift. I'm learning from experience that gripping the shifter knob super hard doesn't help you get it into gear."

Seven seemed to stifle a laugh, but failed miserably. "At least you don't have to worry about anyone stealing it." And then her expression brightened. "Hey, I have something to cheer you up."

"What is it?"

"A cute guy came in last night looking for you."

"You seem giddy. Did you lock him up in the back?"

"No, but that's not a bad idea," Seven admitted.

"Who was he?"

"I don't know—attractive. Think Jim Halpert or Matt Damon but with less forehead."

"Good start," Abby retorted, "but does he read?"

Seven's eyes leaked sunbeams. "That's the best part . . ." She waited as if a drumroll would materialize.

"You're killing me, Smalls!" Abby prodded.

A sweeping motion toward Abby would have to do. " . . . He loves Christmas more than you do!"

"How do you know that?"

"Because he went all yippee-ki-yay over your Christmas display. I'm telling you, I've never seen anyone get so excited about Christmas books—except for you, of course." Seven reached out to clutch Abby's fingers. A vision was apparently blossoming in Seven's head. "You should call him. I think you two would be perfect. I can see it so clearly. You'll start in early October, sipping hot peppermint cocoa every night together at home . . . drinking from each other's cups . . . as Christmas carols play in the background . . . while you watch *It's a Wonderful Life* over and over . . . oh, and little Ralphie will play quietly upstairs in his room. Admit it, it almost makes a person weep."

Abby was definitely not weeping. She followed Seven's gaze but could see nothing. "Ralphie?" she asked incredulously.

"Fine, then, little Kevin," Seven added. She turned. "Oh, I almost forgot. He left you a letter. It's in the register." Seven retrieved it from underneath the till tray and passed it to Abby.

Abby examined the envelope. "Seven, he's from my insurance company."

She offered a shrug. "Yeah, but he was cute—you still need to call him."

Abby tore open the envelope and unfolded the paper. As her eyes leapt sentence to sentence, her nostrils flared.

"What does it say?" Seven asked.

The letter crinkled in Abby's hands. "I'll call him, all right." Her words riddled with anger. "It says they won't pay for my car. It says my insurance was cancelled!"

Carter gripped his highlighter like a knight wielding a sword. While the books spread before him on the table represented but a small fraction of the many Christmas books flooding the market, his college class on Statistical Analysis told him they were enough to provide an in-depth understanding of Christmas stories, their plot, pacing, characters, and more. If he was going to write a Christmas book, he had to understand every part, every piece, how they fit together, and why people purchased them.

He picked up the first, a hardcover, flipped it open, and began to read.

❄

"*No, no, no!*" Abby pleaded. She'd been bounced around so many times already, she tried threats. "If you put me on hold one more time, I swear I'll hunt you down and . . . Hello? *Hello?*"

Too late.

She desperately wanted to slam the phone to the floor but guessed her phone hoped otherwise.

Chest breathe. Tippy toes. Hold. Release. Once more. Chest breathe. Tippy toes. Hold. Release.

As she waited, she scanned the denial letter again.

50

It made no sense because, beside it, she held a copy of Mannie's cancelled check to the insurance company. She had yet to mention the entire incident to her uncle and had no plans to. It would be the death of him.

It has to be a simple misunderstanding, she thought. Then, as she turned the letter over, she read the name of the assigned adjuster. There was no direct number for him, only the 800 number on which she was still on hold—and it continued to spew murder music.

Wait, perhaps there's another way. She pulled open the lid on her laptop, clicked on the search bar, and typed in the man's name. There was more than one match, but it wouldn't take her long to narrow them down.

The words in her head were already plotting.

"Carter Cross," she whispered, "here I come."

Chapter 8

Carter Reads Christmas Books. Read, Carter, Read!

Carter's eyes were bulged and dry. It physically hurt to blink. His head pounded like elves on an anvil. His hands shook like a drunk sailor at sea. The stories were so sweet, he worried his teeth were rotting. But what did he expect, rapidly consuming so many Christmas books?

He was still at the table when Yin wandered in to scour up some breakfast.

"Carter?" His voice rattled off the cupboards with surprise. "Have you been up all night? It's the second night in a row!"

"I've had a nap or two," Carter replied, but with words as frail and sleepy as they were hollow.

"You've got to pace yourself," Yin insisted. "I have two and a half college degrees. I should know."

"It's worse," Carter mumbled. "I still have books left." He picked one from on top of the stack. His face read that he'd rather roll naked in snow than start on it.

When the doorbell rang, wrinkles drew themselves across Yin's forehead. "It's early. Are you expecting someone?"

Carter was already at the door, the unread book in one hand, his wallet in the other. He swung it back to welcome breakfast.

"Good morning, Mr. Carter," said a cocoa-colored El Salvadorian man delivering pizza.

"Good morning, Roberto," replied Carter.

"How many times has Roberto been here?" asked Yin.

It should have been evident. To help dilute the sugar, Carter had been binging on pizza. Never mind that mixing so much sweetener with equal amounts of saturated fat was akin to washing down sleeping pills with Jolt Cola.

As Carter counted out the money, Roberto commented on the book tucked under Carter's arm. "How is that one, Mr. Carter? Any good?"

Carter showed no emotion—may it forever rest in

peace. His words were cold, dead. "It's a Christmas book, Roberto. Nobody cares."

As Roberto wandered away, Yin pushed Carter's books aside to make room for the new pizza box. In so doing, he uncovered a logical question. "Have you considered simply skipping the rest, Carter, and jumping directly into the writing?"

Carter winced, but it was the first spark of emotion he'd shown that day, so they both took it as a positive sign. "Yin, I have to do this right. Skipping ahead would be like reading *Middle-earth* before the *Hobbit*."

Yin's entire face announced that he had no clue what Carter meant, but he wouldn't argue. "But are you learning anything?" Yin wasn't pandering. His curiosity was genuine.

Carter struggled to marshal his thoughts. Perhaps they were confused by toasted pepperoni in the morning. But the longer he pondered, the higher his eyebrows rose.

"There *are* patterns," he said, "common themes I've noticed." His brain strained to summarize them. "Love, faith, home, change." Recognition rose like the sun. "As for characters, I've read about scrooges and saints, innkeepers and shepherds, mothers hoping for children, and orphans . . . so many orphans." He was sitting forward, his tone taking that of a professor. "The plots are shallow, the prose trivial, believability hovers at zero. Oh, and miracles—more Christmas miracles than Santa has sleigh bells." He'd used a metaphor. The pizza was kicking in.

"That's not to say every book is without merit. Dickens was the master, and had the stories ended with his, I'd have no qualms. The problem is the parade of pirates chasing Dickens to his grave, hoping they too can ride a Christmas pony to the Promised Land."

Yin chewed, swallowed, pointed to the obvious. "Carter, isn't that what *you're* trying to do?"

It stopped Carter cold, roped him with chains. He squirmed, shrugged, pushed them off his shoulders. There was no point beating around the Christmas bush. "Yes, I am."

Yin considered one last notion. "Will you be able to do it?"

The words stretched, waiting for Carter to exhale. "We'll soon find out."

❄

Mannie rested on the couch at home, half covered by a blue wool blanket, as the Channel 3 news anchor rambled on in the background about the upcoming Thanksgiving Day parade. Abby hurried in from the kitchen. She had stopped by to check on Mannie on her way to work, but now she was running late.

"How are you doing, Uncle?" Abby asked as she scooted into the family room. "Is there anything else I can get you before I go?"

It was plain he was not a man who cared to be fussed over. "I told you, I'm fine! Just ask everyone at the store to work hard and let them know that I'll be back in a few weeks, as soon as I'm rested."

"Do you need me to fix your blanket?" Abby wondered as she reached to pull it up snug.

"*Abby!*" His glare snarled, and so she left the blanket alone.

She raised her hands in surrender. "Have it your way. There's a sandwich in the fridge—roast beef, your favorite—and I've cut up some carrots and broccoli. They will do you some good, so eat those as well."

"Have a great day!" he answered, half sincerely, half curtly.

Abby stared at the man for a long moment, then dipped down to kiss him on his head one last time before leaving.

Mannie watched the door shut, listened as Abby started his car, waited for the sound of the engine to disappear. He didn't mean to be rude, but he couldn't have her notice: his left arm was numb and aching and his blanket was falling off because he couldn't get enough grip strength in his hands to pull it up tight.

He rested, prayed it would pass, rested longer.

"It's too soon," he mumbled to the empty room as he pressed his fingers against the cushion of the couch. "Please, I need a little more time." His head tipped up toward the ceiling. "There are still a couple of things I need to do."

***

When Carter turned the final page of the last Christmas book, he was certain he heard angels singing the Hallelujah Chorus—and the choir arrived not a moment too soon. One more book and he'd threatened to buy a Red Ryder BB gun and shoot his eyes out. Anything to end the misery.

Now, nearly hypnotized by his blinking cursor, he recognized his fussing may have been premature. When the idea to write a Christmas book had first waved its eager hand, Carter was filled with unsullied excitement. Later, as he trudged through the myriad of Christmas books, digging under the hood to discover what made them tick, that excitement swirled into impatience.

Finally, recognizing that it was time to lay words on paper—sentences, paragraphs, pages—an emotion infinitely more powerful than all the rest clenched its rusty fingers around Carter's heart, threatening to crush him.

Fear.

What if, after all this, he couldn't do it?

Chapter 9

The Christmas Fork

Taking lessons from the books he'd read, Carter crafted his best story about a homeless double-amputee orphan with two hand-carved wooden legs and a crutch. In a soul-wrenching scene, the boy, believing the nativity display at his church to be real, offered his most prized possessions—his two wooden legs—to the manger baby. But when Carter reread his work from the beginning, he wasn't certain whether to weep or to laugh.

He deleted it all and started over, creating instead a story about Santa crashing his sleigh into a chimney, filing a claim, and then dealing with the nonresponsive North Pole Insurance Company. If reimbursement wasn't received soon, Santa would be forced to cancel Christmas.

Carter was fast coming to understand that embellishing adjective-laden accident reports was like a baby's bumbling first step. Finishing a book, even a short Christmas story—crafting a cohesive plot, creating credible characters, inventing interesting dialogue, pulling forward a narrative that would touch a reader's heart—that was running a marathon, blindfolded, uphill and backwards, a feat for which Carter had no training.

It was eight hours later when Yin tapped softly on the door. No pizza had arrived, Carter hadn't come out of his room, and Yin was worried.

"Carter, are you alive?" he asked, pushing the door open.

Carter's eyes were lead, his neck was marble. His arms resting on his pitiless keyboard could have been stuffed with batting. They served only to connect to his lifeless hands and fingers. He was breathing—*in and out, in and out*—but was otherwise stiff as a corpse.

The computer screen was once again blank, save that despicable blinking cursor.

"Did you hear me?" Yin said louder.

Carter stirred. He spoke. "How did Hemingway do it?" he asked, his head rattling ever so slightly.

Although Yin had only read Hemingway in literature

class, he couldn't help but voice the obvious. "I think Hemingway shot himself."

"Before that?" Carter said.

Yin sidestepped the question, dodged it by changing direction. "Do you have *anything* written?"

Carter grunted, letting the disdain in his eyes translate the sound for him.

"How about a title? Start there." Yin spat the words out so easily, as if the likes of said plan had never dawned on Carter.

"Splendid idea!" Carter answered, with sarcasm bleeding oceans. He pushed away from the table. "What do you think I've been trying to do?" he asked. His veins were swollen and pulsing. "I've been searching, brainstorming, investigating different titles for the last six hours. I've even compiled a list. Check it out!" Carter thrust rumpled pages toward Yin before gathering them back to read aloud.

"There are already Christmas books about animals: *The Christmas Cat, The Christmas Dog, The Christmas Pony, The Christmas Mouse, The Christmas Duck.* There are Christmas books about places: *The Christmas Cottage, The Christmas Town, The Christmas Bridge, The Christmas Street, The Christmas Manger.* Nearly every piece of clothing: *The Christmas Sweater, The Christmas Mittens, The*

Christmas Shoes, The Christmas Socks. Chen, even Santa's underwear has been exploited! And let's not forget the never-ending books about things: *The Christmas Box, The Christmas Jars, The Christmas Quilt, The Christmas Sleigh, The Christmas Candle.*" Carter latched onto Yin's arm, pinched flesh with fingernails. His voice quaked with desperation. "I can go on forever! Yin," Carter nearly screamed, "all the best nouns are taken!"

Yin pried Carter's fingers from his forearm, rubbing at the marks that looked like tiny smiles. "There must be something. How about . . . I don't know . . . *The Christmas . . . Monkey?*" Carter didn't move, didn't blink. He wasn't sure if Yin was joking or serious, but either way, it wasn't funny, since he knew *The Christmas Monkey* had already been used.

With no reaction, Yin tried again. "Okay, then . . . um . . ." Yin glanced around the room. "*The Christmas Chair. The Christmas Carpet. The Christmas Spoon. The Christmas Fork. The Christmas Pizza.* Any of those work?"

Carter's jaw dropped open and exasperation dribbled out. His eyes were bulging like a fat man's belly. He'd already done the research. Why did Yin not understand? "The only one of those not already in a Christmas title is *FORK*!"

Yin waited. Carter waited.

With every passing moment, anger simmered into swampy sadness. Soon Carter lifted his head. "Yin?" he asked, so sullenly the walls almost wept. "You're majoring in computer science, right?"

"Currently, yes."

"It's hypothetical, but say I name my book *The Christmas Fork*. How will anyone find it?"

Yin didn't realize he wasn't supposed to answer. Perhaps he didn't hear the word *hypothetical*. "They'd have to search by *Christmas* and also *Fork*, and, well, there are some other search tricks I can teach you to . . ." Yin's mouth kept moving, explaining the finer points of search engine optimization, but all that reached Carter's ears was *blah, blah, blah, blah, blah*.

If presuicidal Hemingway had been there, Carter would have put his arm around the man and his barstool, explained to him that he completely understood, and the pair would have swigged away their sorrows for the balance of the evening—and Carter didn't drink.

Yin must have realized he was being ignored because he started to shuffle from the room. Just before he reached the door, he paused. "You know, it's too bad you can't simply string a bunch of the book names together. You'd totally come up first on Google." And then Yin cackled like the Joker in Batman, but Carter couldn't decide if he sounded more like Heath Ledger in *The Dark Knight* or Jack Nicholson in the version circa 1989.

As he was weighing the two Jokers in his head, Yin's words hung like stagnant smoke that Carter couldn't help but breathe. When he chewed his lips, he could taste it, and then the smoke sparked an idea that flickered.

Carter cranked his head. "Say that again," he demanded.

Yin turned. "I said that if you could put a bunch of the Christmas book names together, you'd search great on Google and . . ."

Carter stood. Carter paced. His arms now flailed. He wasn't bouncing yet, but he was about to. It was a Christmas miracle after all. "Yin, you're brilliant!" he said. "You've just named my book!"

Yin's eyebrows mobilized as one. "*The Christmas Fork?*"

Carter was now laughing. "Fork? No! My book is going to be called . . ." He waited for the words to line up on his tongue. When they finally filed out, they were tap dancing.

"*The Christmas Carol, Angel, Box, Wish!*"

Chapter 10

The Miracle

Mannie punched the numbers on the phone slowly, deliberately. "Doctor, this is Mannie McBride. I noticed you left a message on the machine."

"Thank you for calling me back. How are you doing, Mannie?"

Mannie returned a sarcastic sigh. "At times I'm short of breath. My limbs go numb and throb . . . oh, and, according to you, my heart could give out at any moment. But otherwise, I'm fabulous. How are you?"

He imagined the doctor grinning. "I have a tiny bit of good news," the voice coming through the phone replied.

Mannie sat taller. "I'm listening."

"This isn't a cure, Mannie. The ending will still be the same, but there's a new drug trial that you qualify for. And while I wouldn't classify it as promising—that would raise expectations too high—I think if your heart can hold out, this drug will relieve some of your other symptoms and buy you some extra time."

Mannie had a single question. "How much time?"

He could hear the doctor speaking with someone else. Their voices were muffled. A moment passed before the man answered. "Best guess is two to six months."

Mannie couldn't spit the words out fast enough. "When can I begin?"

"That's why I'm calling. I have the pharma rep sitting in my office as we speak. We've been discussing your case. There will be some paperwork to fill out, but in short, you can start right away. I'll have everything here. Come down at your convenience."

The words stuck in Mannie's throat. It took a moment to jar them free. "Thank you, Doctor."

Mannie hung up the phone, winced, rested, and then punched in the number for a taxi. Once he confirmed that a car was on the way, he attempted to process what had just happened.

His eyes were glassy but brighter than they'd been in days. The muscles in his face that he used to smile received a sudden call to action. He reached for a tissue to wipe his nose, which had decided to run.

While he waited for the ride that would take him to retrieve the drugs necessary to extend his life, Mannie McBride dropped gently to his knees and began to weep.

❄

While a story about a wooden-legged orphan felt overly contrived, and one with a sleigh-crashing Santa who battled an evil insurance company swerved too close to home, a different kind of story was chaining itself together in Carter's head.

It came slowly: a slivered thought here, a slice of vision there. An idea gusted in through a window crack and hung momentarily in the air, free-floating a foot or two above Carter's monitor, daring him to find the right words before it splintered into fragments and faded away forever. It was a serious story that didn't match Carter's whimsical title, but he hoped to eventually link them together.

When Yin pried for details, Carter did his best to summarize. "It's the story of a West Coast trial attorney who is so desperate to win his cases that he spends most holidays at the firm. His wife and two boys pretend that all is well, that life as a family is jolly . . . until their lives fall apart right before Christmas when the mother sits the boys down to tell them that she's moving away."

"It sounds dreadful, very depressing," Yin responded, before hurriedly slapping a hand over his mouth.

Carter didn't object. "Remember, it's fiction," he said, "because nobody in real life would be that heartless." His expression puckered. "But you're right, it is dismal . . . and that's the problem. While it feels like there could be a story in there, I haven't been able to figure out where it goes. It's like my wheels are turning, but the car is stuck in story mud."

"That's a metaphor, right?" Yin confirmed.

Carter nodded. "How do I get unstuck? What am I supposed to do?"

Yin's answer was logical. "I guess you find someone who has a towing chain."

"You're right!" Carter shouted, to confirm what he'd likewise been thinking. "I need someone with more experience to give me some pointers. I'm simply too new at this. Yin—I need a writer, or perhaps a book editor. Someone who knows what they're doing . . . a professional!"

Yin chuckled aloud. "Carter, we live in Springfield,

not New York City. Have you ever known or even heard of *anyone* who's a book editor?"

The question wrapped itself in the silence of the room, a quiet that was torn open only by Yin's waving arms.

"Until we find someone, should we order pizza?"

❄

Mannie waited for Abby to fix his lunch, cover it with plastic, and then kiss his forehead before she left for the store. It was daily déjà vu.

"I have a quick errand to run after work," she said, "but I'll drop back around six."

"No need. I'm feeling much better."

Finally, Mannie wasn't lying. Once she'd gone, he pulled the pills from the bottom drawer of his dresser and headed to the kitchen for water. It was his third day taking the wonder drug, and he was finally noticing a difference. His arms, while still numb, no longer felt frozen. He could walk without limping. He could once again grip a glass of water without worrying that it would break free and plummet to the floor.

Mannie reached for his phone.

"Andrew? Hey, it's Mannie. Listen, can we get together today or tomorrow? I need you to prepare the paperwork to transfer business ownership to my niece, Abby."

Mannie waited as Andrew checked his calendar.

"There's just one problem," Mannie added. "I need to do it without her knowing."

Chapter 11

The Agreement

When the doorbell rang, Carter squeezed from his chair. Why did Roberto bother? Carter wondered. Why didn't he just walk in? They were already on a first-name basis. What was left? Exchanging emails? Spending holidays together?

Ring, ring.

"Coming! Hold your huffing horses."

Carter wove around a pillar of empty pizza boxes. Rather than haul them to the dumpster, he and Yin had stacked them by the front door in a creation dubbed the "Leaning Tower of Pizza."

Carter scratched at the itchy stubble on his chin, then twisted the knob and swung the door open. A split second of recognition was displaced by an afternoon of dread. If this was Roberto, he'd been chugging estrogen by the gallon.

The girl standing at the doorway was shorter than Carter would have guessed from her picture, but he recognized her toasted-hazel eyes and her trademark smile.

"Hello," she said. "I'm looking for Carter Cross?"

Carter's gaze crashed to the floor. His dignity followed. He was wearing tatty basketball shorts and a coffee-stained T-shirt, one that had never known the privilege of meeting an iron. Worse, the room behind him was in shambles, a decorating style he would label Post–Hurricane Katrina. There were third-world garbage dumps that were more appealing.

She either didn't notice or masked it well, and as she extended her hand, Carter debated pretending to be Yin. It would have worked but for that pesky difference in complexion.

"I'm Carter," he heard himself say.

"My name is Abby McBride. Are you the Carter Cross who works for Business Alliance Deposit Insurance?"

How should he answer? She must have noticed his hesitation because her nose wrinkled like a curious bunny's. "Sort of," Carter finally replied. "I'm the Carter Cross who *did* work there. I no longer do."

"But your name is on my insurance claim as the adjuster," she said, as if all he needed was some convincing. It was evident she was trying hard to be polite, like he was that insufferable distant relative at Thanksgiving dinner whom one tolerates out of duty.

Carter didn't want to admit to being fired. "We . . . parted ways. I'm surprised they gave you my address."

It was her turn to look guilty. "They didn't. When I saw your name listed on the claim, I . . . well, I Googled you. I kept getting the complete runaround when I called the toll-free number. They insist I wasn't insured, but I have a copy of the cancelled check and—"

"I'm truly sorry, Miss McBride," Carter interrupted. "I wish there were something more I could do."

Carter watched the twinkle in her eye tarnish.

"Thank you," she answered, but her words were so empty they echoed. She turned, was about to leave when she pivoted back around. "Is there someone I can call at the company, someone who will take the time to listen? It's just that my uncle has been sick and so I'm managing our store alone . . . and with the accident and then the insurance problems, I'm now behind on three book editing projects, not to mention the store's year-end inventory. Any name at all would be extremely helpful."

Her words stopped at his ears. He pushed rewind, then parsed them again.

"Did you say *book editing?*"

"Yes. I do some editing for a publisher in New York . . . you know, on the side."

A growing grin nearly touched each ear. It was all he could do to not hug himself. What were the chances? "Miss McBride," he said, as every word shouted *glory be,* "I believe I may be able to help you after all."

❄

When Lenny opened his car door to head to lunch, Carter was waiting in the front passenger's seat.

"What the . . . Carter? What are you doing here?" Lenny stammered.

"You said we should go to lunch sometime. Are you ready? It's my treat."

Lenny glanced around the company lot, as if certain he'd find a hidden-camera film crew. When he noticed nothing, he climbed inside. "What's this about?"

"I told you, I'm here to take you to lunch," Carter said. "But I'm also not going to lie to you." Carter wrapped his arm around Lenny. "When we get back, I need a small favor!"

The arrangement Carter had worked out with Abby was simple: he agreed to contact the many influential people he knew at the insurance company (Lenny), while Abby promised to use her skills as an editor to take a serious look at his writing and offer some pointers. It was a workable proposition for each.

While he waited for Abby to finish with her customer, he wandered over to the café and sampled André's peppermint chocolate cheesecake. It was a slice of pure paradise, perhaps the best dessert Carter had ever eaten.

"I'm so sorry. I'm running late," Abby puffed as she scooted in across the table.

Carter didn't mind. He was still licking crumbs off both sides of his fork. "Forget ReadMore," he told her. "Call this place *EatMore!*"

Her lips parted wide enough to show teeth before she checked her watch. "Did you hear back from anyone at the insurance company yet?" she asked.

"Right to business—I like that. No, not yet, but I've spoken to my contacts, who are looking into it. I should know something in a day or two. Don't worry. I'll keep my end of the agreement."

She folded her arms. Her eyes offered thanks, but

then he caught her watch-glancing a second time. "Did you bring your story?" she asked, looking up.

Carter pulled a small stack of typed pages from a bag that rested at his feet, then reluctantly handed them across the table.

"They still need a lot of work. This is just the beginning. I've still—"

Her raised hand stopped him. "I won't draw a red frowny face on it, I promise." She peeked toward the door. "However, if it's fine with you, I'd like to read these later when I have more time. My uncle had to go back to the hospital for some follow-up tests, and I need to pick him up."

Carter's shoulders slumped like cheap chocolate pudding. He must have looked like a child on Christmas morning who had just opened Grandma's hand-knit sweater instead of a bike.

His disappointment didn't go unnoticed. Abby swallowed, her head tilted slightly to one side. She raised two fingers. "I take it you need these right away?"

Carter glanced first at his feet before looking up. "I'm sort of stuck with my story's direction and I was . . . well, hoping you'd be able to help."

"And do you really believe you'll be able to help me get some answers from the insurance company?"

He tried to sound confident. "I do."

"I'll tell you what, then," she offered. "If you need these now . . ." But then she paused. The words blinking across her brow read, *Never mind, it's probably a bad idea.*

"What is it?" Carter pressed.

"I was thinking that if you'd like to drive me there, I could read your pages in the car."

"To visit your uncle?"

"He doesn't generally bite. And it's only if you want to. I'm simply trying to make this work for the both of us."

"No, no, no, that sounds great." Carter wiped away his surprise, collected his things, and pointed her toward his car.

For twenty minutes all Carter heard was Abby shuffling pages. He did his best to keep his eyes on the road, but in snatched glimpses, he caught her grin, grimace, and giggle. He wasn't certain if she was laughing with him or at him.

As Carter pulled into the hospital parking lot, Abby turned over the last page. The timing was perfect.

"It's okay," Carter told her, as he shut off the engine. "I'm a turtle. I have a hard shell. I can take the truth."

"Fair enough," she replied. "I'll be honest." She shifted toward him. "Without more, it's hard to see where the story is going. But from what I've read, I can tell you that while it needs a lot of work, I'm willing to offer some pointers to improve it." She moistened her lower lip, perhaps to make it easier for her words to slide out. "That said, I see a glimmer of crouching talent."

He would take it as a compliment, though he could still see uncertainty hanging in her eyes. "What is it?" he pried.

"It's just . . . can I ask you something?" As Carter nodded, her gaze returned to the pages. "Is this fiction?"

"Yes. Why?"

"Tell me then why you love Christmas," she prodded. "You must if you want to write a story about it."

She let the weight of her words draw him close.

"Let's see," he finally replied. "The food is tasty. Everyone gets time off work. People are unusually happy. There's a fat man in a red suit who hands out gifts. What's not to like?"

Her stare didn't move, didn't leave its target. It was apparently not the answer she was fishing for.

"Let me try this a different way," she said. "Are your parents alive?"

"Yes."

"Where are they from?"

"Spokane. Is that relevant?"

"Like the parents in your story," she noted.

"Does that matter?"

"What do you do as a family for Christmas? I presume you get together." Her words blistered when touched. Silence filled the space. It was answer enough. "So you don't go back home?" she confirmed.

"I haven't been back for a couple of years, that's all," Carter conceded. "My parents finally got divorced and . . . things haven't been the same. Why would my parents' divorce disqualify me from writing about Christmas?" A hint of irritation skirted out.

"I'm not suggesting it does. I'm just trying to help you see one of the problems with your writing."

"What's that?"

"If you want to tell a compelling Christmas story, it helps if you believe in Christmas."

"You don't think I do?"

She returned a plastic grin. It must have also been time to change the subject because her next question had nothing to do with his story.

"Shall we go meet my uncle Mannie?"

He followed her inside to the elevator, where she pushed a button for the fourth floor. When the doors closed, he took the opportunity to ask a question of his own.

"Can I ask you something now?"

She turned. "Sure. What is it?"

"It's about your accident."

"Yes?" Her whole frame leaned in to listen.

"You slid on black ice, right? That's what caused you to crash?"

"Correct." Although the fluorescent light in the elevator wasn't particularly harsh, she still squinted.

"And you could see the trees, or rocks, or whatever it was you hit, and you knew that you were going to crash, that it was inevitable?"

"Where is this going?"

"I'm curious about the moment right before impact. In the split second before you smashed . . ." Carter hesitated, but there was no backing out now. " . . . did you smile?"

Her eyebrows drew close as she fit the puzzling words together. "Did I smile?" she echoed. Her foot tapped, but not to any music. "No, as I recall, right before impact I was screaming for my life! Seriously, why on earth would I smile?" She was gazing up with a look that told him it was the stupidest question she'd ever been asked.

What had he been thinking?

Lest she believe him to be a lunatic, he decided to explain. "I've dealt with accidents for years, and I've just

. . . I've heard that people sometimes see their lives flash before their eyes . . . and I . . . I wondered if that happened to you? If it did, and if you've had a good life, I was curious to know if it . . . did it make you smile?"

She stared at him for what felt like an eternity, but it must have been only seconds because the doors opened on the fourth floor. When she didn't move, Carter reached for the button to hold the doors open. It was as if she was trying to figure him out, but the numbers weren't adding up.

When she finally did reply, it was naturally with a Christmas movie line. "You're a strange one, Mr. Grinch."

Carter was about to object, but she cut him off. "Can I ask you a favor now?" she said.

"Sure, what?"

The alarm on the elevator began to ring from Carter holding the doors open for too long. They stepped off together and stopped in the waiting area. Her words all but fell to the floor and begged.

"Don't say anything to my uncle about the problem with my auto claim. Our cars are insured through the business, and if a payment wasn't sent in properly, it was likely his oversight. With his health issues, I don't want him to worry."

He met her gaze, pondered the striking color of her

eyes, then let his own gaze drop to her chin. For the first time, he noticed that she had dimples.

"My lips are sealed."

❄

Instead of finding Mannie in the waiting room as he'd promised, they discovered him sitting in an examination room three doors down.

"What's wrong? Is everything all right?" Abby asked as she entered, distress cresting in her voice.

Mannie's arms protested in disgust, as much as arms hooked to tubes could. "Everything is fine. You know doctors . . . their time is always worth more than everyone else's. They just want to make sure I'm not dehydrated, so they're giving me some extra fluid. It won't be long."

In addition to the IV that poked out of Mannie's arm, a beeping monitor assured anyone entering that the man was still alive. His face was slightly jaundiced, but that may have been nothing more than the room's pasty lighting.

When Mannie noticed Carter, he sat forward. "I'm sorry," he said to Abby, "I didn't realize you brought company."

"Uncle, this is Carter Cross. Carter, this is my uncle Mannie." Abby pointed her finger at the respective parties, as if there would otherwise be confusion as to who was who.

Mannie's head jerked straight. His stare lassoed Carter, then circled back around to Abby.

Abby knew the look, could see what was happening. She jumped in with both feet before he embarrassed himself. "No, Uncle, it's not like that . . . Carter is a . . . well, he's doing some writing and I'm helping him out. We're just friends. That's all."

Mannie shrugged it off, and, with the air clear, they visited. Abby let Mannie know that the shipment of cookbooks they'd ordered had arrived on time and she had already put them out on the sales floor. Mannie reinforced his appreciation for her stepping up while he got back on his feet, and he assured her she was running the store better than he ever did. She told him that Rosa would be directing the nonfiction book club that met on Thursdays. He told her that her hair looked very nice the way she'd pulled it back over her shoulders.

Carter mostly watched, waited, and listened.

A nurse hurried in, checked the IV, then explained to Mannie that it would take another twenty minutes.

"In that case," he informed her, "I'll need you to add some Dr. Pepper to the IV."

The nurse giggled, her chubby body shook, her eyes sparkled. It probably wasn't her first joke from Mannie.

"I'm kinda serious about the Dr. Pepper," he told Abby once the nurse had gone. "Do you mind? Get one for everybody."

Abby had barely left the room when Mannie directed his gaze at Carter. Not really *at* him but rather *through* him, as if Carter were made of glass and Mannie wanted to examine his heart.

"I've been watching you watch Abby," he finally said.

Carter's eyes were metallic. "I beg your pardon?"

"Son, I need to ask you a serious question."

Carter hesitated, then bent in. "Certainly."

"What do you think of Abby?"

Leaning close had been a mistake. Mannie had grabbed onto Carter's arms and wouldn't let go. Should Carter call for help?

"Um . . . she seems like a very nice person."

"Oh, for heaven's sake! Do you think she's attractive?" He let the boy go. His head wagged, as if to say he'd seen granite that was less dense.

"I . . . um . . . yes, she's very pretty. But Mr. McBride,

you've completely misunderstood. I thought Abby made it clear. We're not dating."

"Obviously! Look, I like you, Carter, so I'm going to ask you a favor. I'm wondering if you can help me with something. It's rather important."

"I can try. What is it?"

"First, can I trust you?"

"You don't even know me."

"That's why I'm asking, can I trust you?"

Carter didn't bother pointing out the man's skewed logic. "Yes, you can trust me."

"Perfect. Now, you can't breathe a word of this to Abby."

"Of what?"

"Abby said you're a writer."

"I wouldn't say . . . well, I'm working on it."

"Good enough. Carter?" He motioned him closer, waited until his mouth was inches from Carter's ear. "You never know how these hospital visits will turn out, and just in case things don't go as planned in the long run, I'd like your help in writing my obituary. Can you do that?"

"Your obituary?"

"Yes, it's the summary of one's life they print in the paper when—"

"I know what an obituary is, but is it going to be

necessary? For you, I mean? And if so, wouldn't Abby be the one—"

Mannie's words sliced Carter's sentence in half, stopped it cold. "She'll say that it invites negativity. I don't even want to go there with her. I'm asking *you*. Will *you* help me?"

Steps tapped on the tile behind them as Abby slid into the room. "Paging Dr. Pepper. Dr. Pepper, please come to the examination room," she joked as she passed canned drinks to both Mannie and Carter.

"I see where she gets it from," Carter quipped.

Abby took it as the compliment it was meant to be, then turned around to place her wallet back into her purse. With her back turned, Carter silently raised his can to Mannie. He'd made his decision. His lips didn't need to move. As his head nodded, his eyes did the talking.

"I will."

Chapter 12

Money and Hugs

Carter was at the computer making changes to his story when his phone rang. Caller ID politely informed him that it was Lenny.

"Carter, I've got some answers for you on the McBride claim—but be warned, it's a little complicated."

"Talk to me," Carter said.

"It turns out there are two policies."

"Two?"

"Yes. They're a small business, so, as you know, the cars are registered in the business name."

"Nothing wrong with that."

"That's correct, but in addition to the auto, Mr. McBride took out a life policy thirteen months ago."

Carter's eyebrows lifted. "Life insurance?"

"Yes, and here's the problem. When he sent in his payment, he wrote one check for both policies but apparently only wrote one policy number on the check. It meant the entire amount was applied to the life side, which put his auto policy into default."

"But we would have sent him a notice of cancellation?"

"Which we did. That's where it gets tricky. When he received his notice of nonpayment, he called up to complain. He spoke to Jennifer in billing in the Providence call center. I pulled the tape and listened to the entire conversation."

"And . . . ?"

"Jennifer noticed the problem and told him that she would fix it, that he was paid up on both policies, and to disregard the cancellation notice. But either the system glitched or she didn't apply it correctly because the payment never transferred over to the auto side."

Even Carter's phone was nodding. "So he *was* covered?"

"Sure, he sent in the payment on time. It's definitely our mistake. I've already sent it to processing, and they've just sent over the check. The car is a total, so they've paid out the entire claim. I've signed off and I'm putting the check in the mail to her now."

"Lenny, she'll . . . well, she'll need it right away. I'll swing by and pick it up for her since I'll be seeing her later today." Carter didn't have to see Lenny's face to know his mouth was hanging open.

"Wait, you two are dating?" Lenny asked, but as a statement, not a question.

"We're just friends."

A low laugh crawled through the phone. "Holy moly! You're dating. Good for you, Carter!"

"So, what about the check?" Carter asked again. "It would sincerely help her out, and we'd both owe you." Carter was spreading on the charm so thick, Lenny would need a knife to scrape it off.

Carter could almost hear Lenny's shaking head. "Thing is, I can't let you drop it off since you aren't an employee any longer."

"Lenny, come on. What am I going to do, throw on a wig and try to cash it? You know me better than that. The thing is, I need to impress this girl, and this is your chance to help me out—and when do you want to do lunch again, Friday?"

Lenny hesitated for only a moment, but it was long enough that Carter knew he had him. "Excellent. I'll swing by right now and pick up the check. Oh, and Lenny . . . one last question."

"Yes?"

"The life insurance policy. You say it was opened a little over a year ago?"

"Yes."

"Did he have a checkup? Was there a physical submitted as part of the application?"

"Of course, there would have to be. We won't write a policy that large without one."

"That large? Do you remember the amount?"

Carter heard a ruffle of papers as Lenny looked it up. "I have it. Are you ready?"

"Go ahead."

"If Mr. McBride dies, his heirs—in this case, his niece—will get a check for half a million dollars."

Carter drove by ReadMore, glanced in the front window from the street to make absolutely certain Abby was working, and then headed directly to Mannie's house. It was a white Cape Cod with cedar shingles, dormer windows on top, and a large chimney flanking each end.

Carter knocked twice before Mannie finally opened the door.

"Carter?" Wrinkles wrapped Mannie's eyes. He checked his watch.

"What are you dying from?" Carter asked, skipping the customary *hello*. His words couldn't fly straighter. "How much time do you have left?"

Mannie turned sideways, letting the questions slip past. "What are you talking about?" he asked, but the understudy in a third-grade play could have done a better job of acting.

Carter spelled it out for him. "At the hospital, you said you watched me watch Abby."

"So?"

"You weren't the only one paying attention. She mentioned that your hospital visits are the result of fainting spells. When we walked out that night, I noticed you were favoring your left arm. You were clenching your jaw trying like crazy not to let Abby see you limp. You asked for help writing an obituary, and then I learned that just over a year ago, you took out a life insurance policy. You may be able to sell Abby on a tale about low blood sugar, but I'm not buying it."

Mannie's frame sagged. It seemed he was out of words and sick of pretending. This time when he turned sideways, it was with a sweep of his arm to steer Carter inside. The two men rested together on the couch.

"It's kind of a relief," Mannie finally said, "having it out on the table, not needing to hide it."

"What do you have?" Carter asked.

"Amyloidosis. You can Google the specifics, but the gist of ol' Amy is that she's a party girl and my organs, most notably my heart, are party central. The type I have is called *light chain,* but there's nothing light about it."

"Is there anything they can do?" Carter wondered.

"I'm past that, Carter. I'd like to think I'm reaching the acceptance stage."

"Why haven't you told Abby? That doesn't seem fair. Doesn't she have the right to know?"

A stillness draped the room, as if the entire home wanted to hear what Mannie had to say. "Carter, you'd need to have grown up with the girl to understand. She lives for Christmas, plans for it all year. She always has. She starts listening to the music in October, makes her lists in early November, cries during every cheesy Christmas special all through December. You could say she loves Christmas the same way that flowers adore sunshine. If I break the news to her now, it will completely ruin not only this Christmas but every single one to follow. I won't have her being sad on my account every year—year after year—when her favorite day rolls around. Do you understand?"

Every word was unwavering. Every inch of the man was determined. "Yes, sir," Carter answered.

"Then you need to promise me, Son, with a Holy Bible, swear-on-your-grave type of promise that you won't tell her. Can you do that for me?"

Was there truly a choice? "I promise."

"Thank you."

"So how long do you have?"

For a man with little time, Mannie was noticeably calm. "They first said I'd be dead by Christmas. Then, out of the blue, my doctor discovered a trial drug that should give me the time I need to get ready. Let me ask you a question, Carter. Was that a coincidence, or was it a miracle?"

Carter's shoulders lifted. "I don't know."

"Do you believe in miracles?" Mannie asked.

Carter edged forward. It gave him more time to think. "I guess they're possible. I mean, I think they're feasible. I just feel like too many people call things in their lives miracles that don't rise up to meet the qualifications. Does that make sense?"

Mannie had also scooted forward. "I hear you, Son. You and I are not much different in that regard. But I'm telling you, I was going to be dead, and that's all Abby would have remembered on her favorite day of the year, and so I looked at my ceiling and I asked aloud for that not to happen. And the next day when the doctor called, I can tell you that in that sliver of a moment, it felt an awful lot like a Christmas miracle to me."

"When do you plan to tell her?"

"I hope I have until January, perhaps February."

"There's one more thing I need to ask you," Carter added.

"Sure."

"The life policy."

"Yeah, how do you know about that?"

"I worked for the insurance company. That's how I met Abby. My colleague there says it was taken out a little over a year ago. When were you diagnosed?"

"In October."

"I'm confused, then. Did you know when you took out the policy that you were sick?"

"If I did, then that would have been a preexisting condition and the company wouldn't have written the policy, right?"

"Are you saying it was luck?"

"I'm saying that after I'm gone, Abby isn't going to have to worry about the store doing well to pay her bills. I'm saying that if she wants to pick up and move to Zimbabwe to raise giraffes, she'll be able to do that. And to that end, I hope my brother and his wife are proud of the job I've done."

Carter pressed. "Did you have a feeling something was wrong?"

Mannie stepped around his words. "It felt like I needed to be better prepared, and so I did something about it. I guess that takes us back to the very same question, doesn't it?"

"What's that?"

"Would you call that a coincidence or a miracle?"

It was the third time Carter sat down with Abby at ReadMore, let her read his work, tried to implement her suggestions, marshaled as much information about the writing process as would stick. He told her that she'd been kind to take the time. Would she be as considerate, he wondered, once she knew her insurance claim had been settled?

He tried to not watch her as she read, the way her tidy white teeth tugged at her lower lip, the way she tapped her pen in circles around troublesome words. Sometimes he couldn't help himself.

"This is much better, Carter," she said, handing his pages back. "Your story is not nearly as gloomy."

"What you're doing is very helpful."

"Carter, I'm an editor. Hand me a Bible and I'll mark it up for improvement."

She was right. He'd learned that, as an editor, she could be brutal. Yet, though she always scribbled across his work like a disgruntled teacher, he couldn't remember a time when he'd been so excited to take criticism.

His eyes raised a hand. "If that's true, if a story can always be improved, how will I know when to stop?"

Abby surveyed the store. There were currently no customers. "Here's how I see it," she explained. "There are mechanics to writing—grammar, punctuation, style. These decisions are constant: should I write a short sentence or a long one? Should the story be told in first person or third? Would it be better in past or present tense? These choices cumulatively shape the finished product. Within these hundreds or even thousands of decisions, many are mechanical, like where do I put the comma? Do I join two sentences with a comma or a semicolon? These can all be mastered with a little time and practice."

"Or, in my case, a *lot* of time and practice."

"Perhaps. My point is, they can indeed be learned and conquered. But there is another side to the writing equation that gets tricky: the esoteric side. Those decisions are harder to teach. I find they are more innate."

"Give me an example."

"Like knowing when a story is ready. You have to be able to visualize your finished product, grasp what you as the writer are trying to say, and then repeatedly sculpt it until it matches or exceeds your vision. It's important to be able to know when it's ready, and it's equally important to know when it's time to stop."

"Will I ever get it?" asked Carter.

"I doubt it," Abby answered, holding a serious expression for as long as her lips would allow. "Hemingway said it aptly: 'We are all apprentices in a craft where no one ever becomes a master.'"

Carter scribbled the quote in his notes. Then, as Abby stood, apparently finished for the day, he made an announcement. "Abby, come with me. I have a surprise for you in my car."

Abby honestly hadn't minded helping Carter. He'd been improving and seemed genuinely grateful. She waited while he fished an envelope from his car's center console. When he turned, a goofy smile was pinned to his face.

"Now that we're finished for today," he said, "I have this for you."

He sounded like a game-show host passing out contestant prizes, and Abby half expected a spotlight to swing over and a studio audience to spontaneously clap. As she reached for the envelope, it slipped from her fingers to the ground, and she stumbled into him trying to pick it up.

To ease her own tension, she attempted to make a joke as she tore at the flap, still unsure what was inside. "And the winner is . . ." Except it wasn't very funny and he didn't laugh. She assumed that he had bought her movie tickets or perhaps a department-store gift card, but instead she noticed a check—a very large check—from her insurance company that would more than cover the cost of her deceased Fiesta.

"My insurance money?" she asked, which was a silly question because it was self-evident, but it was also unexpected, and she was so overjoyed at the possibility of not having to drive Mannie's stick shift any longer that her voice cracked. "It's more than my car was worth!" she exclaimed, sounding like a pubescent teenager.

"That part wasn't me," admitted Carter. "You should thank Mannie. He had the policy rider that pays out a claim with a car that's a model year newer. Normally I'd suggest it's not worth the cost, but Mannie's been . . . lucky."

Red-faced, and without really considering her actions, Abby reached both arms around Carter, forgetting how much broader his shoulders were than her smaller limbs, and she tried to offer a thankful hug.

It should have been a harmless gesture, except that her brain was flashing a warning signal to her arms that hugging a man so unexpectedly would not be completely proper. Her confused muscles froze mid-motion as an internal argument ensued.

Hug the guy! He was kind enough to bring you this massive check, demanded the spontaneous side of her brain. *Are you crazy, girl? Back off or he'll think you're into him,* screamed the reserved side.

Then an unexpected memory opened, a moment from when she was tiny, perhaps four or five, standing in a supermarket checkout line with her uncle. She reached up and wrapped her uneasy arms around his protecting leg, not noticing until seconds later that her uncle Mannie was standing two people ahead in line as she clung to the leg of a complete stranger.

The result of that trauma, coupled with her current indecision, translated into a hug for Carter that was not only halfhearted but lopsided. It was as if she'd leaned her body close to his, extended part of an arm, and then decided to have a brief nap.

"I'm so sorry, Carter," she said, pulling her arms away. But her face was now close to the color of stewed beets.

For anyone watching, the boyish grin now attached to Carter proclaimed the moment as the most memorable he'd likely had in months. He followed by draping her with kind eyes. "That was my fault," he admitted. "I shouldn't have surprised you like that. I'm sorry."

And then he bent close and gave her a proper token hug, like she'd tried to give him, before pulling away as if nothing unusual had happened. Then, as casually as one could possibly imagine, he turned and politely asked, "When are you going to look for a new car?"

And in a fraction of time so fleeting she was not sure what its measurement might be called, Abby was put completely at ease, and a warmness rose in her chest that could best be described as savored sips of André's dark chocolate cocoa.

After mutual thanks were again exchanged, Carter climbed into his car and drove away. Abby, in turn, strolled toward the door to find Seven holding it open.

"That was entertaining," Seven said. "Rosa and I were watching from the window."

"I don't know what you mean," replied Abby.

"Girl, I've watched the National Geographic channel, and that was surprisingly similar to the mating dance of the red-capped manakin."

"Seven!"

But for the rest of the evening, as Abby shelved books, she quietly hummed a medley of her favorite Christmas songs.

Chapter 13

Get Closer

Harold Rotterdamm, district manager at Business Alliance Deposit Insurance, appeared at Lenny's desk so abruptly it almost caught both men by surprise. When he spoke, his voice floated above the cubicles, as if even the furniture understood that he was the man in charge.

"Lenny, do you have a moment?"

Lenny immediately quit typing. He pivoted, stood. He would have saluted had he thought it was appropriate. "Yes, sir. How can I help?"

"You trained Carter, right? You two were friends?"

Lenny wiped his brow. "Yeah, I guess so. Is he in trouble?"

"When did Carter begin to embellish his accident reports?" His packed words almost rubbed shoulders.

"I . . . um . . . I'm not sure. Perhaps a year ago. Why?"

"That's helpful. Can you go back and pull a copy of the descriptions from his assigned claims for the last year and then forward those to me?"

"I guess so. Is there a problem?"

"Thanks, Lenny. One more thing . . . I don't know if you still speak with Carter or not, but don't say anything about this conversation. Someone from corporate will be contacting him. I'll let you know if there's anything else."

※

"Will you please listen for the door?" Carter asked Yin. "I'll be upstairs."

While it was true Carter was waiting for Abby, he wasn't calling it a date. He had simply agreed to tag along to help her find a car.

Whatever it was called, the result was an apartment that shimmered, a testament to the value of urban renewal when a tenant takes ownership.

When the bell rang, Yin answered. "Hi, you must be Abby. Carter will be down in a minute. I'm Yin, his roommate."

Abby shook hands, then followed him inside. She was halfway to the couch when she peered across the room to a series of photographs hanging on the wall, artistic close-ups of curious geometric shapes oozing saturated colors.

"Hey, are you ready to go?" Carter asked, turning the corner.

Apparently she wasn't. Her index finger was raised and she was pointing. "These are terrific. Where did you get them?"

Carter herded a sheepish stare toward Yin, asking if she was teasing. Yin shrugged.

She focused on the picture in the middle. "I love the lines in this one," she said, "and the vitality in the color."

"I'm glad you like them," Carter replied, deciding not to tell her they were his. He would just shoo her out the door and they could be on their way—until Yin piped up.

"Carter took those!"

Abby froze, twisted around. "Seriously?" she exclaimed. She leaned in to study them like an art student might study a Renoir. "I didn't know you were into photography. Where did you take these?"

Carter hesitated, then surrendered. "That one on the end . . . you've seen it before," he told her.

She slid down to the last picture. "No, I'm certain I'd remember."

"Look closer," Carter suggested. Perhaps this was a fun game after all.

It took her nearly a minute. "That's the inside of a car, right?" But she didn't seem certain. She tossed confusion around like a volleyball.

Carter pointed toward the picture's edge. "Not just any car. Look more closely."

Her eyes glistened like shiny quarters. "Wait! Is that *my* car?"

Carter tried to hide his satisfaction, but it bolted free. "It was the only thing that kept me sane at my old job. I'd take them at the tow lot."

Abby let her finger trace the photo's lines. "They're breathtaking. I would never have guessed there was such beauty in something as ugly as a car wreck."

"It's why I enjoy it. They're unexpected. It's something tha—" His words halted mid-syllable. Carter's brain was reminding his mouth that it was straying into areas too personal.

"Please continue," she begged. "I'm very interested."

Carter bolstered his words and tried again. "It's a simple lesson that I believe the photos teach."

"Yes?" she prodded.

"As an adjuster, all I saw all day were accidents

disrupting people's lives. To make sense of them, I found that getting close helped."

"What do you mean?"

"When we run into a problem, we're often taught to step back, to take a broader view. I guess I'm not certain that's always good advice. Stepping back doesn't make the problem go away. Instead, to find purpose, if there is such a thing, at times we need to get closer—painfully close. If we do, we can find beauty."

For a moment, no one spoke. It was a stillness that for Carter became unnerving. "That's cheesy, I know," he added. Every word was packed with apology. "It's just something I've been thinking about."

Abby gripped him by the wrists, waited for his eyes to lift. She was no longer looking at his pictures. "That's rather amazing," she told him. "Can you write that up in a short paragraph for me?"

"What? Why?"

"I want to place it below your pictures."

"I'm sorry, I don't understand."

"Your pictures, Carter! If I hang these in the store and post them on the store's Facebook page, I'll sell a bunch of them. Are you interested?"

Lenny was ducking beside his car when Carter approached.

"I got your message, Lenny. What's so important?"

"Get in! Quick!" Lenny stammered. Even in the cold, drops of sweat channeled down his temples. He was flushed, he was shaking, he was a complete mess.

Carter climbed inside. Lenny followed. He was still glancing about, as if the mafia had put out a hit order and he could be gunned down at any moment.

"I can't let Harold see me," Lenny explained.

"Is Harold following you?" Carter wondered, glancing back. "Why would Harold be following you?"

"He's not, but I can't take a chance. He told me not to tell you, but after much thought, I've made the decision that if we're now friends, then . . . well, friendship has to come first."

Carter had the urge to check Lenny for a fever. The Lenny he knew would rather boil in scorching oil than go against Harold.

"Lenny, what's wrong?"

"I don't know, but something's going to happen, and I wanted to warn you. Harold asked me to send him copies of all your . . . your embellishments, your accident descriptions, for the last year!" Lenny's eyes bulged. "I had to, Carter. I had no choice!"

Carter tried to calm the man. "Relax. It's okay, Lenny. Why does he want them?"

Lenny was dripping. "He wouldn't say, but I heard him talking later to someone from legal and Carter, he was furious! I'm not sure, but they must be planning some action against you! That's all I can imagine. I knew you shouldn't have embellished."

Carter half smiled. "Accident embellishment in the first degree?" he mocked musingly. "I don't think it's a capital crime."

"Carter, don't make fun. They're a big company. If they want to cause you legal problems, how will you fight them?"

It was a smile that soon slid away. Lenny had a point. "I'm sorry, Lenny, you're right. I guess it's my attitude that always gets me in trouble."

"I simply came by to warn you, to give you a heads-up. And Carter . . . ?"

"Yes, Lenny?"

"No matter what they do to you, you didn't hear it from me!"

Chapter 14

The Visitor

Carter arrived at Mannie's right at ten. He'd been coming every Tuesday and Thursday, when the two men knew that Abby was working.

"Did you look over the list I sent?" Carter asked.

"What list?" Mannie answered.

"I sent it by email. It's the suggested obituary guidelines I found online."

"Sorry, I haven't logged in today. Can we look it over now?" For a dying man begging for help, Mannie seemed to be in no hurry.

"Sure, I guess." Carter pulled it from his folder. He started at the top. "These are the items typically found in an obituary."

Mannie leaned in with his pencil. "I'm ready."

"It says you should start with the basic information: name, dates, cause of death, a list of loved ones."

Mannie set his pencil aside. "I don't need the Internet to know all that!"

"I'm just reading the guidelines. After that, it suggests that you list a few of the things that you have accomplished in your life . . . you know, the items you'd put on a resume."

"It's a bit late to be applying for a job."

"It's customary to—"

Mannie cut him short, blindsided him with bluntness. "Are you suggesting I tell people how wonderful I was?"

"Why not? I'm pretty good at it. Give me a little free rein and I can make you sound rather impressive. What do you say?" It was a question that at least deserved a shrug. "No? How about special interests, then?"

Mannie's words slapped again at the table. "I was especially interested in raising Abby. Does she count? Can't we just talk about her?"

Carter scanned the balance of the list. There was nothing about including nieces. "I don't think it's customary to—"

"Did I tell you about the time I took Abby to

Yellowstone and she tried to pet a bear?" Mannie asked, not letting Carter finish.

Every visit with Mannie was the same. It was hard to keep him focused, though Carter would admit the tangential stories were amusing. Of course, he would never say a word to Abby.

"Can I ask you a question about Abby?" Carter said.

Mannie nodded.

"Why isn't she . . . attached?"

Mannie reached for a tissue and blew his nose. He waited until he and Carter could lock eyes. "She's had her share of boyfriends."

"She has?"

"Tons of them. Let me see, there was Larry, the physician. He was a while ago. The relationship started out well, but as a dermatologist, Larry was overly sensitive, took everything personally. I think he needed a thicker skin. After Larry, there was Steve. He was an editor, like Abby, and I had such high hopes for them."

"Why didn't it work out?"

"He followed *The Chicago Manual of Style* and Abby used the *AP Stylebook*. It was like they were from different religions. In the end, they were never on the same page."

Carter raised a disbelieving finger to interrupt, but nothing slowed down Mannie. "I guess after Steve there was Peter, the science teacher. That relationship was more of an experiment. Then there was Raul, the architect, except he was way too structured. Corbin, the banker, was nice. Sadly, after a while, Abby lost interest. Then, Kevin, he worked for a temp agency. He only stuck around for a few weeks."

Carter quietly mumbled. "And that, kids, is how I met your mother."

"Say what?" Mannie asked.

"I said I think you're making these up."

Mannie's glare bumped Carter in the chest. When the man spoke, his words were soft and low, hovering barely above the ground, forcing Carter to strain.

"Carter, listen to what I'm telling you: Abby's had her heart broken, just like you. And I suppose she's broken her share of others' hearts. I can't tell you why Abby is single at the moment any more than I can say why *you're* still single. What I can tell you is that she's beautiful. More important, you'll never find a girl with more love packed into one courageous soul. Abby is loyal, loving, smart, and selfless, and she makes everyone around her better." Mannie's body tightened, his neck and arms flushed, his lungs filled with air. "As I see it, Carter, there's only one question."

Carter inched forward. "What's that?"

The room was still as stone as Mannie leaned in to meet Carter.

"What are you going to do about it?"

❋

Yin watched from the safety of the table as Carter paced the room like an expectant father. "I don't understand the worry," Yin said. "You've already been out with Abby a bunch of times. How is this any different?"

Carter all but bit his nails. "We've been out, but we haven't been *out.*"

Yin parsed the words in his head. "It may be a cultural thing," he said, "but I don't get the difference. Is that why she's driving?" Every word was shrugging.

"No. She wants to show me her new car—and before tonight we've only been out as friends."

His explanation didn't help. "Aren't you *still* friends?"

"Yes. No. I don't know. It doesn't matter. How do I look?" Carter faced Yin like he was facing a magic mirror, waiting for it to speak.

Yin sensed a trick question. "Am I supposed to say *handsome?*"

Carter wasn't really listening. "My hair looks goofy, doesn't it?" There was no good response. His words strangled themselves with frustration. "I'm going to go fix it. Holler if the doorbell rings." Before Yin could answer, Carter dashed from the room. He was halfway up the stairs when the sound of the doorbell bounded in.

"She's early!" Carter whispered as he rushed back down the stairs. Anxiety flushed in through every crack and crevice as he stepped toward the door. Then, as if by magic, the horror and despair washed away like poor quality paint in the rain. Underneath, self-assurance stepped out of hiding.

Carter opened the door as gallantly as possible to find there was indeed a woman waiting on the porch. She was elegantly dressed, wearing immaculate makeup, and later Carter would have to admit she was rather beautiful. At the moment, however, his head was playing connect the dots, and the resulting picture was a jumble of mixed-up lines.

The woman interrupted the process. "Does a girl have to stand out here all day, or are you going to be a gentleman and invite her in?"

A single word pried open his mouth. "Mom?"

❄

Carter's mother, Lorella Cross—soon to be Lorella Penton—was a woman of slight build with a thin neck and long legs. Her generous brandy eyes drew attention away from the wrinkles invading the fringes of her cheeks and jaw. Tonight she smelled of fresh flowers, pressed clothes, and confidence.

When Carter realized it wasn't Abby on his porch arriving early to show off her new car, he called and delayed their date by half an hour. He was not merely a basket case, he was a Native-American, grandma-made, fully hand-woven baby-carrier basket case. He and his mother sat beside one another on Carter's bed.

"Do you want me to read you a story?" she said, poking him with playfulness.

"Mom, stop it! That's not funny." Carter stood, trying to swallow his concern. "You shouldn't be joking—and you should have called to warn me you were coming."

She ratcheted up her volume knob a notch. "Carter, I did call. I'm still waiting to hear a reply from my last two messages. I came in person because I'm getting married in a little over two weeks and I'd sincerely love it if you could be there. I thought that coming here, talking face-to-face, letting you meet Joel, might make a difference."

Carter's words choked. "He's here?"

"I had him wait in the car. I told him you're a little freaked out by all of this, and he completely understands. He's a good man, Son. You'll like him."

"Oh, splendid!" His words were so sopping with sarcasm they almost dripped.

"Carter, I know the yelling, the fighting, the divorce, it was hard for you and your brother. I get it. It's only worse now for you because you've never accepted it. I think you always believed your dad and I would get back together."

Carter brushed fingers numbly across his hair, hoping to straighten his thoughts. "It's just so weird thinking you'll be living with some strange guy," he said. "It doesn't make sense."

Lorella tied on a smile. "You always were the romantic in the family, bruised as you may be. I think if you meet Joel, you'll see that this is a positive thing."

While each word was wrapped with resolve, boxed tightly with conviction, Carter couldn't bring himself to pull at the ribbon. "I'm not sure I'm ready, Mom."

She licked disappointment from her lips, then started slowly. "I can respect that. But will you come out for the wedding, meet him there, give him a chance?"

"That's another thing. Why are you getting married three days before Christmas? What's up with that?"

"We thought it was a marvelous idea. Family would already be in town; people wouldn't need to take extra time off. Besides, we'd like to be married by Christmas. It will be perfect."

"Here's a better idea. Wait until next Halloween. It's more appropriate." The words came out withered, perhaps because he was only half joking.

She laughed or at least faked it, but the empty moment that followed stretched across the room to cover everything. When he finally spoke, it was mostly to himself. "I just don't need another reason to hate Christmas." He regretted speaking the words aloud, tried to force them back into the box in his head from which they'd sprung. Oddly, they no longer fit.

Lorella jerked upright, clasped her son's hands. "Hate Christmas? Carter, you don't hate Christmas. That's silly."

When his frown didn't surrender, she pulled him back down to sit beside her.

"The first time your dad and I separated—when you were younger—it was right before Christmas, and for that I'm sorry. It's why I came back, why I tried for so long to make it all work. But I won't sit here and listen to you say that you hate the holiday, because that's not true. As a small boy, Christmas was your favorite," she told him.

He inhaled a pause. "What are you talking about?"

"It's true. When you were seven or eight, you and I

117

would spend hours decorating the house for Christmas. You loved it!"

"I don't remember." His words whimpered. "Where did you meet Joel anyway, a bar?" Carter asked, changing the subject.

Lorella giggled like a tickled child. "Carter, you're hysterical," she said. "Actually, I met him in a biker gang. We were at the same tattoo parlor when I was getting a skull inked onto my chest . . . right after we'd pulled off that bank robbery."

If she was trying to make him queasy, she had hit pay dirt. "*Mom!* That's enough," he protested, flailing desperate arms that begged for her to stop.

She didn't. "Truthfully, we met at church."

"Church?" The word was a stranger. "Since when do you go to church?" he asked.

"I went as a little girl. I guess I simply got out of the habit later in life. After the divorce, one of the benefits was that I found my way back."

Her words flew out with such confidence, such self-assurance, Carter couldn't help but take notice. "I guess that's what bothers me," he said. "You seem so okay with all of this—the whole divorce thing. It's a bit unnerving."

Lorella leaned in with love. "Carter, everyone is dealing

with it but you. Just come out for a visit. You'll see that it's all going to be fine—better than fine. We've missed having you. We worry about you." She hesitated, then fished in her purse and reeled out an envelope. She handed it to Carter. "I even brought you a plane ticket, so, no excuses. Can I count on you being there?"

His one-word protest bazookaed out. "*Mom!*"

She was ready. "If you don't use it, no problem. But I hope you do."

Before he could answer, the doorbell interrupted. Yin hollered the news up to Carter from the bottom of the stairs.

"Abby is here!"

Chapter 15

The Offer

Carter tried to hold open the car door with confidence as he waited for Abby to climb in behind the wheel. He hurried around to the passenger's side and then let the silence settle in long enough for both to enjoy the new-car smell.

To celebrate Abby's purchase, they'd decided to go out for German food because, according to Rosa, it was never a bad choice.

Carter's pre-date jitters had proved pointless. Sitting beside Abby now, he felt warm and comfortable—even playful.

"Have you read any good books lately?" Carter asked, interrupting the moment with interested eyes.

Abby pulled her gaze from the road, directed her squint momentarily in his direction. When she looked as if she hadn't understood, Carter clarified. "It was one of the suggested questions for first dates that I read online." He followed it with a smirk. "Then again, since you've been reading my book—at least as much as I have written—it may not be the best choice to start."

"I see," Abby said, letting her smile chase his. "First-date questions from a website. That should make for interesting conversation. What are my other choices?"

"Asking about your favorite holiday was on the list, but I think I know that one already. We could move on to your hobbies and interests."

"Then I should answer suitably," she declared.

"What do you mean?"

"I'm told that the energy of all first dates is spent trying to impress the other person enough to garner a second, so I need to be proper about it." She cleared her throat. "Let's see, my interests: I adore salacious discourse with fascinating people, delicious films that make me think, and inventive books that make my soul fly. Was that eloquent enough?"

Carter was nodding. "Impressive. Next, I'd like to hear how you'd describe yourself to a stranger."

She gave him a subtle wink, laughed without missing

a beat. "That's easy. I'm a low-maintenance girl but with high-maintenance hair." She pulled forward in the seat and shook her head to settle her curls.

"I've noticed that much already," Carter continued. "I guess now tell me about your faults."

"Faults?" Abby asked, letting the conversation screech to a halt. "Was that really on the list? That's a terrible site. It's way too early for faults."

"Sorry, I just threw it in to mix things up."

"I see. Well, I'm looking for a therapist who can help me with my adjectivious obsession. Can we count that?"

"No, but you get points for your sense of humor. Next—"

"Sorry," she interrupted. "It's my turn now. Have you always wanted to be a writer?"

It didn't sound like a question from a website, and the way she kept glancing at him made it appear as if she was truly interested.

"I've always been intrigued by the way writers craft sentences," Carter began, "but deciding to write a book was . . . we'll call it *unexpected*."

"I can tell you that your talent has come a long way from insurance embellishing."

Carter's head swiveled. A question slid across his brow, caused it to wrinkle.

Abby didn't wait for him to ask. "The insurance company called me yesterday," she explained. "I spoke with lovely Louise in customer service, an extremely pleasant woman. She was making a follow-up call and seemed surprised that I hadn't received a copy of the accident report. She said they usually send a summary with the settlement check. Since I didn't receive it, she was kind enough to email the complete report right away."

"The long one?" Carter confirmed, his voice stumbling. "Those are usually never sent out."

"I must be special because it was sent to me. Let me see if I can remember the phrasing," she said, as the night's teasing light reflected off her polished teeth. "*Lightning ripped the sodden, sleeting clouds like they were pieces of two-dollar fabric.*" She giggled as the words bubbled out.

"I'm turning a sunburned red, aren't I?" Carter asked.

A finger touched her lower lip. "I'd say it's more tomato."

"Descriptive writing was about the only thing there that kept me sane. As you've probably figured out by now, they fired me over it—though I still prefer to call it *creative differences.*"

"You *were* creative. I'll give you that."

"Yeah, but I imagine you think a guy who gets fired is a . . . loser?"

"For what you did? Not at all. I did some editing once for a woman who was a stay-at-home mom. When she reentered the workforce, she wrote on her resume that she'd been a *Domestic Engineer* who had *manufactured* four children. She listed that she'd been their *direct supervisor* and was responsible for their *annual increased output.*"

"Did she get in trouble?"

"Trouble? It was all true! They hired her. That's the point. When creativity focuses on the positive, it's an art. Embellishing doesn't mean lying. Liars are plentiful, Carter. Good communicators are hard to find."

"But I was fired."

"I think the key, as with perhaps everything in life, is knowing where to draw the line."

They arrived at BetterWurst, Rosa's favorite German restaurant, and on opposite sides of the most delightful dish of sauerbraten that either had ever tasted, they discussed both writing and dating questions in equally healthy proportions.

Then, to Abby's delight, as an encore, Carter took her to see the Christmas light display at Forest Park, nearly three miles of twinkle heaven. She couldn't have beamed brighter, and to top it off, he bought her hot cocoa, which they sipped together in the car, careful not to spill.

"You've been quiet for a spell," she said. "You must still be contemplating my charm."

"This is terrible to admit on a date, but I was actually still thinking about my mother."

"Probably not the answer most girls want to hear."

"It's just so bizarre. I can't let go of the fact that my mother is marrying a stranger."

"She seemed awfully nice, at least for the moment we spoke on the porch. I think she's right . . . you should go to the wedding. You'll regret it later if you don't."

"I feel like I need more time."

Abby blew on her hot cocoa, as if she hoped for a moment to craft her words. "Possibly, or perhaps you need to get closer to the situation to see the beauty. It's a trick a friend of mine taught me."

Carter held up his fist, waited for her to bump it. How could he argue?

"Hang on," she said, as she set down her cup and reached into her pocket. "I know another way to cheer you up. Give me your phone."

"My phone?"

"Now! Hand it over."

She placed it beside hers, pushed buttons, transferred

files. It took only a few minutes. "There you go," she said, her grin wide. "You now have a playlist of all my favorite Christmas songs. Not to mention that I changed your ringtone to 'Santa Baby.' I guarantee you will never be sad again."

"You didn't!" he said. But her face clearly indicated that she definitely had. "You're a little crazy when it comes to Christmas, you know that?"

"Mannie reminds me of that frequently."

"Why is that?" Carter asked. "Why do you love it so much?"

"The truth?"

"Absolutely," he said, though actually, if he could keep watching her lips, a lie would be perfectly fine.

"Perhaps I've *decided* to love it," she answered matter-of-factly.

His head tilted right. "Decided? What does that mean?"

"I just think in today's world, it's easy to be cynical. It takes effort to look past the negative and proactively seek out the good. For me, it's meant deciding to love the holidays."

Carter's escaping scowl looked unconvinced. "Fair enough. I guess I get that," he answered, "but what if the goodness is an illusion? What if the world is simply a cold

126

and bitter place? Isn't choosing Christmas hiding from that reality?"

He read her eyes. They told him there wasn't a pretty way to say certain things. She straightened in her seat. "First of all, the world isn't always cold and bitter. At times it's warm and wonderful. Second . . . let's pretend you're right. It means I can face reality and be miserable, or choose what you suggest is an illusion but live a happier life. Thanks, but I'll stick with Christmas. Don't you agree?"

He could barely convince the answer to rise above his throat. "I guess I'm still figuring that out. My mother said as a boy I used to love the holiday. I don't remember it that way, but I trust she's telling the truth."

She patted him confidently on his leg. "Then we'll call you a doubter who sometimes believes, and I'm a believer who sometimes doubts. We're not that different. It means there's still hope for you, Carter Cross. There is still hope for you. If that's true, the night has been charming and I think I'm ready to try out your theory."

"Which theory is that?"

"Come a bit closer, Carter. Tell me what you see." Her stare tipped into his.

"I see a crazy girl," he quipped.

She wasn't laughing. "Get closer, then. Now what?"

"I see . . . a tiny freckle on your cheek."

"Closer," she whispered. A few inches separated them.

He could feel the heat of her breath. He was about to speak, but their noses touched. As her lips pressed his, Carter closed his eyes. Instead of darkness, he saw teeming colors—true, dependable, loyal, and alive colors. Crimson, auburn, plum, cinnamon, magenta, indigo, mango, and gold—so much gold. He wished that he had words deep enough to describe the warmth that was filling him inside. When their lips pulled apart, when his eyelids lifted open, the images fled, but the light remained.

Abby's eyes opened next. She stared back at him for a moment, perhaps curious at the questions she seemed to read in his gaze. She didn't offer answers. Her finger instead touched his lower lip and then lingered. "Don't say a word," she finally whispered, with words scarcely there. "Let's try that again!"

"Good morning. I'm calling for Mr. Carter Cross." The woman's voice reaching through the phone was formal, businesslike. She sounded oldish, but it was hard to tell.

"This is Carter. How may I help you?"

"Mr. Cross, my name is Janice Cumberford. We met once, at corporate training, when you were first hired by Business Alliance Deposit Insurance. I was with the legal department. I helped teach a session on Business Ethics. Do you recall?"

Legal department? Business Ethics? Lenny wasn't kidding. "I recall attending the class, but I'm sorry, I don't remember you specifically. How may I help?"

Carter could hear the woman shuffling her papers.

"Bear with me and I'll explain," Ms. Cumberford said. "When an employee is terminated at the company, the supervisor must document the reasons for the termination. It's company procedure to cover our legal liabilities. Do you understand?"

Not at all. His stomach twisted. "What does this have to do with me?"

"When you were terminated, Mr. Cross, your manager, Mr. Rotterdamm, sent in several of your accident descriptions as prima facie evidence that his action was justified—which, of course, it was."

"Prima what?"

"I apologize. That's my legal background coming through."

Carter's feet spread wide. His stance broadened. He glanced around for a pen in case he should need to document the communication. His voice deepened. "Look, am I being sued or something? What is this all about?"

"Sued?" Her reply flowed with confusion. "No, no, Mr. Cross, you misunderstand. I'm no longer in legal. I head up the HR department now. When Mr. Rotterdamm sent your descriptions over, I'd remembered you from the training. Mr. Cross . . . we'd like to offer you a new position."

The room percolated puzzlement. "You want to hire me back?"

"Not as an adjuster. I think we can both agree you are not exactly suited for that. Rather, I'd like to bring you on as our Public Relations Liaison. It's a position created after the acronym debacle of '98. The liaison writes press releases for the company, approves brochure content, oversees our marketing materials, that sort of thing. You're good with words, Mr. Cross. You'd be a natural. Anyone who can describe something as horrific as a car accident with such beauty, that's a person we need in our PR department. The communications team works out of our Sunnyvale office. That's where HR is located. You'd be on the floor right above us."

Was this for real? Carter wondered. "Sunnyvale?" he asked.

"Yes, in California. Near San Jose, south of San Francisco. It's a beautiful place to live. Superb weather . . . oh, and Sunnyvale was recently named the Safest City in America."

"Safest?" repeated Carter, not meaning to speak it aloud.

"Very safe, and a tremendous opportunity. I'd like to fly you out to meet Michael Lowe. He heads up the department, but we've already talked, and it's merely a formality. The position pays . . . well, I'll send you all the information via email, but I think you'll be pleasantly surprised. Does this sound like an opportunity that would be of interest?"

Carter chased his breath. "I . . . this is unexpected. When would the job start?"

"As soon as it's convenient for you to make the move, but we were hoping within twelve weeks. Real estate here can be tight, but we can provide temporary housing until you find something permanent."

"And you said Sunnyvale?" Carter confirmed.

"Yes. Safest place on earth."

Carter's words loitered while his head measured the possibility. Cued by the silence, Ms. Cumberford continued. "I don't expect an answer today. I just wanted to make you aware of the opportunity. I have your email and I'll send more details. Look everything over, and if it's a position you'd like to consider, give me a call back by the end of next week and we'll fly you out to discuss it further. How does that sound?"

"That sounds . . . thank you."

Once the call had ended, Carter checked his phone's log. He Googled her number to make sure it wasn't a prank. Sure enough, the company had offices in Sunnyvale. His next call was to Abby to share the news. He pressed send to connect, but thought better of it and immediately hung up. Things were going well with Abby. He really liked her. If he took the position, it would mean moving three thousand miles away.

As he did his best to weigh the prospect of moving, one word wouldn't sit quietly: *Safe!*

Was it time to play it safe, or did he need to take a risk?

Carter paced. Yin waited on the couch. He knew from experience that a volley of questions would soon be landing nearby. It was verbal ping-pong, and he was ready to play.

Carter served. "Help me out here, Yin! What should I do?"

"It's a job. The pay is fabulous. It's in California. How can you pass it up?"

"I know, but I'm finally getting to know Abby. She kissed me. How can I leave?"

"You'll turn down a life-changing opportunity for a kiss?"

"That's not what I'm saying. I hope there will be more. I like her, and I don't want to simply walk away from a meaningful relationship for a job."

"Then invite her to go along."

Carter's hands hurled sideways. "Yin, she owns a store! Her uncle is sick. She won't be going anywhere!"

"When is your lease up?"

"Not until June, but I have the right to sublease."

Yin's arms folded. "But Carter, who'd want to live with me in this dump?"

Carter swiveled. "Are you kidding? You obviously haven't read my ad." He motioned toward the north wall. "You know how at night we can sometimes hear the rattle of big trucks on the expressway?"

"Yeah."

"That, my friend, is *easy freeway access that will have you at work in no time.* And the avocado shag carpet in the back that probably hasn't been replaced since the '70s?"

"Don't remind me."

Carter's finger pretended to follow an imaginary advertisement he was reading midair. *The quaint retro decorating style in this lovely apartment embraces an almost grandmotherly charm."*

Yin was quick to clue in. "That means it hasn't been updated since the old hag died and it still smells just like her, right?"

Carter was barely getting started. "You know the steep stairs to the bedrooms?" he asked.

"How could I forget?" Yin confirmed.

Carter waved like a game-show sidekick highlighting lovely parting gifts. *This cozy abode has an upstairs that will absolutely take your breath away! "*

"It's true!" Yin chimed, his pupils wide. "You're terrific, Carter! I can see why they'd want to hire you."

"There's one more," Carter insisted. "The apartment also comes furnished with the world's most incredible roommate, a man who will help you stick to your diet."

Yin's bobbing chin stopped. "What are you saying?"

"I'm saying," Carter continued, as his lips tugged into a grin, "that *he'll always be there to eat at least half of the pizza."* Carter stood tall. He turned to Yin. "Seriously, you've been the best friend one could hope for, and if I take this job, I'm going to miss you."

Yin nodded his thanks. He wasn't one to get emotional. "Is there anything else that would keep you here, then, besides the girl and your brilliant roommate?"

The truth could be stabbing. "I guess not."

"My mother always says, 'A bird does not sing because it has an answer. It sings because it has a song.'"

The game stopped. Carter scratched at his hairline. All remaining questions bounced to the floor. "What does that even mean?" he asked.

"I think," answered Yin, "it means you need to go talk to the bird."

Chapter 16

Plato and Play-Doh

It took exactly four minutes from the time Mannie pressed '*request*' for the driver from the ride-sharing service to pull up in front of the home—a feat Mannie found remarkable. It was the first time he had used the app that Abby had loaded onto his phone, and he was stunned by its efficiency. He didn't even have to explain to the driver—a coffee-drinking man with thick fingers—where to go. The address had already been transmitted magically to him online shortly after Mannie had punched it into his own phone. Why, the trip was even prepaid, and as the man drove, Mannie couldn't quit shaking his head. He was indeed living in, as Aldous Huxley had noted in his classic novel, *a brave, new world.*

Eleven minutes later, with no traffic at such a late hour, the car slowed to a friendly stop in front of the ReadMore Café.

"Are you sure you want to be dropped off here?" the driver asked, his question crusted with concern. "It's the middle of the night. The store is closed."

"It's fine. I'm meeting my son here. He's a police-man."

It was a lie, of course, and whether it was believed by the harmless driver didn't honestly matter to Mannie. Besides, what was the worst that might happen? A mal-content would jump from a dark alley and take Mannie's life? *Get in line! You're a little late!* Mannie mused to him-self as he climbed out, slipped his key into the store's lock, and then methodically marched inside.

He wouldn't eat a dessert from the display, wouldn't touch any books left sitting on the counters, wouldn't disturb anything in the back room. Short of Abby watch-ing the store's video surveillance footage in the morning, which she'd have no reason to do, Mannie didn't want her to know he'd been here.

His wasn't a visit to check up on things, to make sure his niece was properly running the place. He suspected she was doing a stellar job of that. This visit was—how would he put it?—a reckoning of reality. For a man facing his imminent demise, what better place to reconcile the meaningful moments of his life than where much of the adventure had started? Mannie had come to the ReadMore Café at midnight to think, reflect, and consider.

He pulled a stool from the front near the register to his favorite spot toward the back where the main bookshelves intersected—travel, history, fiction, and how-to. Was there a more glorious place in all the world?

Where else could a long arm reach books on Plato and Play-Doh, fashion and fascism, Hemingway and Rachael Ray?

"So many books and now so little time," he said aloud. But he didn't intend this to be a session to simmer in self-regret. That wasn't why he was here.

He straightened.

No, this was instead a personal pilgrimage—albeit a short one—like in *The Canterbury Tales* or *The Pilgrim's Progress*. Granted, if he'd had more time, more opportunity, less responsibility, no disease that was pilfering away his existence, perhaps he would have gone on a *true search* to discover life's *real* meaning in a place like Mount Kailash in Tibet or Char Dham in India. He'd certainly traveled to many similarly exotic locations as a single man, before Abby had been thrust into the picture.

He rocked forward on his stool.

Was that what this unsettling midnight search was about? Was he hoping to reconcile harbored regret? His head shook. He wouldn't admit to such. Then what?

Answers.

Contrary to what Mannie had told Carter, the notion of writing his obituary had caused some reflection. He simply hoped now, after a tiny bit of introspection, to uncover a smidgeon of understanding, an end-of-life resolution. In short, before dying, he wanted to feel at peace.

His questions were simple: Had his life mattered? Was he satisfied? Was he ready for what was to come next—and what might that look like? They were the normal kind of questions any dying man might wonder about while sitting alone in a closed bookstore at quarter past midnight.

"Is there more? Is there a purpose for the life I've lived? Please let there be more!" Mannie whispered, this time to the walls, the shelves, the surrounding stories.

Mannie had never been a religious man and in fact had seldom set foot inside a church. The questions he needed answered, as near he could tell, seemed equally relevant no matter his surroundings. While most people prayed for answers, Mannie often chose an alternative method. He turned to the pages of his books.

In the hours that followed, Mannie perused Shakespeare and Socrates, Rousseau and Thoreau. He even cracked open the good book of Psalms and read several chapters attributed to David.

It was all interesting, informative, imaginative, and, to a degree, soothing, but it was nothing he hadn't read before, and the verses didn't provide the depth of comfort he'd hoped to uncover.

Finally, an hour before dawn, exhausted, waving a white flag and ready to return home, Mannie carefully put away each retrieved volume, replaced his stool to the front—careful to return it exactly as he had found it—and then he opened the app on his phone and requested his ride home.

He waited in the dark near the door, motionless but still empty, chained to longing as he watched for the driver who would arrive in four and a half minutes—if he believed the numbers counting down on his app.

He shifted his weight. He twisted slightly.

Perhaps there were no real answers in books or elsewhere. Perhaps there was no true purpose to this crazy existence called life. And then Mannie cast a glance back toward the only light still left on in the store. It was the sole security light, a single fixture in the pocked ceiling of square fluorescent boxes that remained constantly on, day and night, to always make certain that the store was never left in total darkness.

Yet it wasn't the lone light casting its embracing glow to the floor and fixtures below that caught Mannie's attention, that had locked his feet to the floor and kept his neck twisted in curiosity. It was that he'd just noticed that the light hovered, like a lone illuminating sun, directly above Abby's familiar Christmas book display.

It was a towering thing, stacked from a solid yet diverse foundation, each story distinct, but each whispering a familiar strain:

Joy to the world. Peace on earth. Good will toward men.

Mannie had come tonight hoping to find answers in books that might address his apprehensions—and as he pondered the beams breaking past the darkness to dance across the multitude of Christmas covers, the hard wrinkles wrapping his tired eyes softened.

A pair of headlights turned the corner, pulled up to the storefront, and stopped. The waiting car honked.

Mannie twisted back around, pushed open the glass door, listened to the bell sound, and waved his hand at the driver to motion that he'd be there shortly. Then he locked the door and walked to the awaiting car—this one driven by a thin man whose head was loosely wrapped with a checkered bandanna—and he climbed inside. The driver didn't ask Mannie what he was doing in that part of town so very early in the morning. He didn't seem to care. And as the car pulled away, Mannie couldn't help but focus on the store window and wonder.

Like a lighthouse in a raging storm of darkness and fear, the shining glow radiating to the world from inside the ReadMore Café had never been more meaningful. The trailing light even reached its warm fingers through the car's back window as it raced away, light that seemed to voice words.

"Have peace, Mannie! All is well! Peace and good will toward men."

❄

Carter pushed out the words. "Abby, there's something I need to tell you."

"What is it?"

"I've been offered a job."

"Carter, that's awesome. With who? What type?"

"Mostly writing—press releases, articles, brochures,

corporate stuff. Surprisingly, it's with the same insurance company I just left. It's a different department."

"It sounds like something you'd enjoy."

Carter nodded. "It's an unbelievable opportunity. I'd be the company's communication spokesperson." As he explained, he tried desperately to read her reaction. "The problem is that I'd have to move to Sunnyvale."

Abby's head turned. Was she casting a look of concern or curiosity?

"California?" she asked.

"That's where the job is located. I've been emailing the recruiter in HR. They want me to fly out and firm everything up as soon as possible. They're offering a salary that is nearly double what I was making."

"Well, that . . ." Abby's words paused for a moment midsentence. " . . . that sounds amazing."

If he was hoping she would drop to her knees and with tears beg him to stay, he was disappointed. In Carter's head, however, thoughts were scrambling to take sides. On the left, romance rallied emotion. On the right, realism circled reason. The leader of each drew a sword.

Explain to her that you're falling in love, Romance demanded. *Tell her that you can't live without her.*

Realism laughed. *You unemployed FOOL! This is a*

rare opportunity for you to finally do something you love!
You can't pass this up. Invite her to come along if you must.
If she can't, know there are plenty of other beautiful women
in California.

Metal clanked against metal. Carter could smell the
sweat, almost taste the blood.

"Carter?" Abby was flapping her hand. "Are you listening?"

"I'm sorry, what did you say?"

"I said that if you took it, I would miss you, but I
would also never want to stand in your way."

"If I do, will you come out . . . for a visit?" he asked,
but with words so unsure they wilted.

"Sure," she answered politely. "When will you decide?"

"I have to let them know soon."

"Okay, but let me know when you do because I have
another application pending."

"Application?"

"Yeah! For a boyfriend. A girl has to have a backup
plan."

He'd hoped talking to her would make things easier. Had she just called him her boyfriend? With a raised
brow, with romance and realism still in open combat, he
watched her do something that caused them both to stop
and turn.

Abby reached for Carter's cheek, let the soft tips of her fingers brush along the surface of his warm skin, held his face in her hand long enough to gaze for a lingering moment into his eyes, then bent close and kissed him alluringly on the lips.

Chapter 17

Rename Jane

Carter punched in his mother's number, hung up before it could connect, then growled aloud and dialed her again. This time he held his breath and waited.

It rang once . . . twice.

When her message began to play, Carter high-fived air and praised heaven. Leaving a message would be so much easier.

"Hi, this is Lorella Cross." Her tone was so bright Carter needed sunglasses. "I can't take your call at the moment, but please leave your name and number and I'll ring you back as soon as possible. Good-bye, now!"

Carter was wet around his neck. "Hi, Mom. It's Carter." He felt like he was calling in sick for work when he knew he'd be spending the day on the beach. "Listen, I'm not going to be able to make it out for the wedding. I'm sorry and I simply wanted to let you know. Maybe I can come out in early spring. I can meet Joel . . . er," Carter said his name but instantly decided it wasn't right. "James . . ." he continued, but he knew that wasn't right either. "George?" he finally stammered sheepishly, as if the recording would correct him. It sounded like he was playing *Name-the-Beatles*. He tried to save face. "You know who I mean . . . your new husband." He was flustered by his mistake, how it would sound when she played it back. Perhaps that was why, as he was about to hang up, his lips engaged one more time on their own without first checking with his brain. "Give my best to Dad."

It was too late to retrieve the words once they'd escaped, and if he could have flogged himself for his stupidity without it hurting, he would have.

"The comedy show is over," he finally mumbled, her machine still recording every syllable. "There's nothing more to see. 'Bye, Mom."

And he hung up.

Carter sat on a wooden stool at the counter beside Abby, praying that customers would shop elsewhere today so he and Abby would have more uninterrupted time to talk. So far it had been working.

"You've been giving me pages of your story," she said, "but I haven't heard a title. Are you keeping it a secret?"

His timid words barely plied their way out. "I have . . . one idea, I guess . . ."

"Spit it out."

"Yin came up with the approach. I was thinking of calling it *The Christmas Carol, Angel, Box, Wish!*"

She was stoic. *Make a note to never play poker with Abby.* Then the edge of a smile pushed through.

"I see a grin, but I can't tell what type?" he announced.

"As an editor," she replied, "I can tell you that titles are important. So let me ask, what does it mean to you? What do you think about when you hear it?"

He didn't hesitate. "It makes me laugh."

"You appreciate the sarcasm?"

"Who doesn't? What about you? What do you think of the name?"

Her mouth opened but then closed. It meant she was thinking. "It also makes me laugh—and yes, I too appreciate sarcasm, if it's offered up in the right serving size.

But it's more than that. It's a name that likewise reminds me of my favorite Christmas books."

"Does that mean you like it?"

"I like how it reflects varying views of the season. Some will see only the humor. But I hope others will see that in addition, it mirrors the reasons so many love the holiday. It's a name that will—like Christmas itself—let people choose what they take away."

"Is everything to you a metaphor?"

"Does a stitch in time save nine?" She blinked owlishly.

"I think metaphorically that means, yes."

He kissed her on the cheek, but it merely served to encourage her.

"There's something else I've been thinking about that I'd like to discuss," she added. When she sat taller, he followed suit. "I've been thinking about something you said in the car when we first met."

Now she had his interest. "Truthfully? What?"

"You said you're a turtle, that you have a hard shell, that you can take rejection. Is that true?"

"Are we breaking up?" he asked, causing her lips to half curl.

"Don't be silly. Here's where I'm going. I'm working on a manuscript for a writer and she told me today that she didn't expect to ever have it published—and it made me sad."

"Why is she writing it, then?"

"She said it was only for fun . . . but I think she's kidding herself. I've had the same conversation with scores of other writers. Their chance of being published is miniscule, as is yours, Carter. But rather than embrace the possibility of failure, they tell themselves they don't want to be published because they're scared of the pain and rejection. I wonder if it's smart."

"It sounds like human nature," he said.

"Likely, but shouldn't human nature also push us to hope, to take chances? Let's look at it this way. Do we really need one more Christmas story?"

"Are you talking about my book?" he asked.

"Sure. Does the world need Carter Cross's Christmas book, or do we already have plenty?"

His palms turned up. It was a hard point to argue. "There *are* already thousands of them. I've discovered that much. Perhaps more than one person could ever read."

"So why do we keep writing them?" Every word carted a question mark.

"This is more about philosophy than writing, isn't it?" His whole body tipped toward her. He couldn't help himself. Her dimples were working overtime.

"It's why I love my job," she said. "Writing is a metaphor for life. Every year, we—the human race—write thousands of books. I would suggest it's because we thrive on creation. We're wired with a craving to matter, to make a difference. So while it's true there are plenty of books already—Christmas or otherwise—there's a constant need for more hope in the world, more love, more enlightenment. If writing and reading stories help us to achieve that, even to a small degree, then perhaps we can never have enough." There was a softness strapped to her voice.

"So I should keep writing?" Carter asked.

"Suggesting the opposite would cause one to wonder how many Jane Austens or Albert Einsteins or Billy Joels or Oprah Winfreys didn't reach their dreams because they were too afraid to get hurt?"

Sun broke through the window, added warmth to the moment. "Is that my lesson for the day?" Carter asked, gathering up his notes.

"Yes it is," she said. "Embrace failure!"

Carter stood with open arms. "Embracing!" he exclaimed. "Finally something in this conversation that I can get my arms around."

Had Carter not spent time with Rosa, Seven, André, and the rest of the staff at the ReadMore when stopping in to get Abby's writing help, he may have assumed all bookstore Christmas parties to be dull and utterly forgettable. After all, wouldn't they consist of librarian types sitting around sipping milk as they discussed their favorite lines from Dickens?

Instead, Rosa was dancing on the counter in full period costume, recreating a scene from *The Berlin Stories* by Christopher Isherwood, the work that had inspired the movie *Cabaret*. Everyone else's arms were linked, and they were all laughing, circling, watching Rosa as she sang, waiting for her to belt out a key word or phrase—currently the word *marvelous*—at which point all would reach to the center counter for a waiting shot of André's eggnog. It was a race to throw it back without snorting or spilling and then slam the empty glass to the counter while yelling *Kabarett!* in their best sultry-German-girl accents. The last one to do so lost the round, sat, and the game continued.

Not surprisingly, Carter was the first one out. But he was oddly content since it was one of those games in which watching was truly as much fun as participating. Besides, who knew full-figured Rosa could dance and sing?

He parked himself beside Mannie, who had feigned an ankle injury so he could peacefully observe, and only he and Carter knew why.

Mannie watched with reflection, Carter with amusement. Minutes passed before Carter grasped the irony: Carter was experiencing their game *Eggnog Shots*—an apparent tradition—for the very first time, but for Mannie, it was his last.

Once everyone was *eggnog-logged,* as Seven made all repeat ten times, they gathered in a circle on the floor for a game Abby called Rename Jane. It was a game she'd devised using Jane Austen novels—but one that quickly spread to other classical works—in which the book titles were twisted into creative alternatives. The made-up titles were written on slips of papers and waiting in the middle of the circle in a large ceramic bowl.

"The game is simple," Abby explained. "A person selects a paper, reads the name, and then has ten seconds to yell out both the correct book and author. You garner a point for each answer, and as long as you guess correctly, you continue to draw. If you miss either the title or the author, then the turn moves clockwise to the next person. We'll start with Seven."

Abby scooted in beside Carter. She wouldn't be

playing but would serve as the final judge for any disputations.

Seven drew the first paper and read: "*The Art of Getting Men to Read Jane Austen Novels.*" It was confusing, having Jane Austen's name in the fake title, but only for a moment. "I believe the real title is *Persuasion,* also by Jane Austen," Seven said, and she was right. Everyone laughed, including her new boyfriend, Rick Levin, whom she'd brought along to the party.

She proudly drew again. Her next was harder. "*No Babies Made,*" Seven read. It took her longer than the first, but she still yelled out her guess with time to spare. "It's *Men without Women* by Hemingway!"

She scored again and drew her third, "*The Condensed History of Portland and Miami.*" The gleam in her eye said she thought this one would be easy. The expiring time soon confirmed that it wasn't. Her boyfriend gave her hand a squeeze and then took a shot.

"Would it be *A Tale of Two Cities,* by Dickens?" Rick asked. He was a graduate student in engineering, unquestionably smart, and when Abby confirmed he was correct, a glance crossed between Rick and Seven—an exchange best described by anyone watching as an endearing mix of surprise and satisfaction.

Rick's next challenge was more difficult. He read,

"*Did Anyone See Where My Dog Went?*" Time passed with no answer, and so the turn passed to Mannie. Although he didn't guess correctly—the correct answer being *Across the River and Into the Trees* by Hemingway—it remained Mannie's turn since that title had been a free guess for Rick's selection.

But then Mannie schooled everyone on how the game was played.

He picked *Grandpa Bought a Yacht,* and promptly nailed it with *The Old Man and the Sea.* His second read *Hunting for Rude Fowl,* which he correctly solved as *To Kill a Mockingbird* (a turn everyone called too easy). And though his third try took a few seconds longer—*Very Late Schoolchildren,* for which he answered *For Whom the Bell Tolls* by Hemingway—it was during his fourth turn that Rosa accused him of cheating. The fictional title read *The Earl of Deep-Fried Ham Sandwiches,* and, with steeled control, Mannie waited until the last moment to blurt out *The Count of Monte Cristo* by Dumas.

By his fifth turn, the group began to cheer him on. Amidst the praising, Carter leaned to Abby. "I guess it's one benefit of owning a bookstore."

"True," Abby confirmed. "That, and having a master's degree in English Literature."

Her words spooled out, waited for Carter to make the connection.

"English Literature?" he repeated. "What was his undergrad degree?"

Her words almost eye rolled. "English, of course."

"So I'm guessing he writes pretty well?" Carter asked, but he already knew the answer.

"Very!" she confirmed. "It's where I get my love of editing."

Carter turned back to watch Mannie, but with a silent question rising, one that would have to wait for another day, when he could corner Mannie alone. It was a question about why an accomplished writer needed help from an amateur with his obituary.

Mannie continued. His next paper read *The Newest TLC Special about Midgets,* and he guessed *Little Women.* Next, it was *Good-bye Appendages,* which he matched to *Farewell to Arms.* He was not stumped until *Boxers Lack This,* for which he groaned when he learned it was *Sense and Sensibility.*

It was Rosa's turn next, but even before she read the title on her paper, she belted out a laugh so deep and constant it appeared she may have forgotten how to breathe. She'd been sitting beside Seven and Rick all evening, but when she turned sideways, it was as if she'd barely noticed them together. As she laughed, she held fleshy hands tight against her stomach, hugging herself until words wedged out.

"Your name is Rick Levin!" she announced, pointing through her hilarity at the poor man, as if he didn't already know. She thrust her finger in his direction as if it were loaded and he may want to take cover.

"Yes," he confirmed.

"That means if you two marry . . ." It looked like she was going to die of the giggles before she finished. " . . . her name will be *Seven Levin!*"

It was obvious that someone had had too much eggnog.

By now Rosa's tears had joined in the fun, and as they rambled down her cheeks, they took as much mascara with them as they could carry. Everyone in the room was soon laughing, more at Rosa than at her revelation—and through it all, Carter could simply wipe at his eyes and admit that this was the best Christmas party he'd ever attended.

As expected, no one came close to catching Mannie, who was declared the undisputed winner. The night ended with more of André's desserts that mercilessly begged from the table to be poked with a fork and eaten.

"Has everyone got their dessert?" Carter asked, as he

dolloped cream on a crusted tart baked with sugar plums and currants.

It was Seven who answered first. "His or her," she replied.

"I'm sorry, what?" Carter asked.

"I believe what you meant to say was, has everyone got 'his or her' dessert?" Seven explained. "Your pronouns should agree."

Rick, who'd been rather quiet for most of the evening, must have been feeling comfortable because he chimed in next. "I don't claim to be an expert, but wouldn't it also be better to say, 'Does everyone have' rather than 'Has everyone got?'"

Abby hadn't appeared to be listening but must have been since she piped up next. "Yes, and I would suggest that dessert should be plural, not singular, since Rosa has more than one."

It was Abby's instant wink that conveyed they would *never* correct a stranger. Like it or not, he had officially been accepted into the *tribe*. Carter faced the group like a man facing a firing squad, except he was holding a cream-laden tart.

His reply was quick. "Improper grammar!" he declared with a shot. "No less at a bookstore! Ain't nobody got time for that!"

Laughter filled the room again like warm sunshine, and it took minutes before the place approached a level of quiet. When it did, it allowed Mannie, seated two people away from Carter, to hear Rosa's question.

"Carter, have you made a decision about the job?" she asked as casually as nosy-mother-Rosa was able.

Carter's head shook. "Not yet."

Mannie straightened, stood, edged closer. It was a question that seemed to have knocked the wind out of him. "What job?" he asked directly.

Carter fidgeted. When his words finally surfaced, they were tiny and far away. "I've been offered a job in Sunnyvale."

Mannie's twitch joined in. "California?"

A joke lined up on Carter's tongue, but he swallowed it. "Yes."

"How long have you known about this?"

"Several days. I'm considering the position, that's all," Carter explained to him.

The grilling ended as quickly as it had started. Mannie grunted without uttering another word and stomped away. And despite the uncomfortable moment, when Carter drove Abby home, he had to admit it was the best time he could remember ever having with friends.

"That was seriously one amazing party. Thanks for inviting me," he said to Abby.

"We've already sold one of your pictures. How could we not invite you?" she answered. "But let me ask you a question."

"Sure," he replied, assuming it was about his photography.

"Something's wrong with Mannie. Did you notice him tonight?"

Glaciers melted before Carter finally spoke. "Not really. He was probably just tired."

She seemed surprised he didn't see it, nearly begged for understanding. "No, it's more than that. It's like he's worried about something—and when he handed out Christmas bonuses, he was almost teary. And Carter, I saw Rosa's. It was double what Mannie usually gives."

"I don't think it's anything unusual," Carter said. "It's nothing to worry about." But as soon as he spat out the words, he wished he could reel them back.

"I'm telling you," she repeated, "there's something wrong with Mannie, something that he's not telling us. Carter, he's hiding something!"

Chapter 18

The Reveal

Carter Googled Sunnyvale and was pleasantly surprised. While there was nothing on the city's website about an award for safety, they rightfully boasted about everything else. The average summer temperature wasn't too hot—71 degrees; the average winter temperature wasn't too cold—51 degrees. There were restaurants and shopping centers, movie theatres and parks, golf courses and tennis courts. It was close enough to a big city—San Francisco—for convenience, but far enough away to still retain its small-town charm. Carter was waiting for the pages to roll off his printer when the phone rang.

"Carter? This is Mannie. Listen, can you come an hour earlier today? Abby's taking me to visit a friend, and

I want to make sure you and I have time to finish. Plus I'd like to hear more about this California job."

Carter checked his watch. "That'll be perfect because I have something I'd like to discuss with you as well."

"I think we've got the obituary all but wrapped up, but I need your help picking out pictures of Abby. I've found two obituary websites that will allow extra photos. Since Abby is my greatest accomplishment, I want them to be of her."

Carter glanced at the photo taped to the edge of his computer, the picture he'd kept of Abby ever since he had found it in her car.

"I'll be there, and I'll bring a picture also. The one I have is perfect."

When Carter dropped the obituary file onto Mannie's coffee table, Abby's photo slid out. Mannie stooped over it, picked it up. He looked like he was about to comment, but Carter didn't give him time. "Mannie, you told me that you needed help writing your obituary." He aimed his words between Mannie's eyes.

Mannie shot back a puckered scowl, like he was about to be arrested—or worse, shot. "Yes."

Carter squeezed. "Abby told me that you majored in English, that you're a terrific writer. So I ask, what am I doing here?"

Mannie's hands lifted; they waved a white flag. "Fine. Truth is, when a guy is short on time, he has to cover his bets. And for me, that means Abby."

"Explain!"

Mannie rocked back into the couch. It was a full surrender. "I needed to know you better, to be sure about you. I needed to see if I was going to have to haunt you from the grave."

Carter's voice rose. "Are you? Because that doesn't sound very pleasant to me."

The query was interrupted by the squeaking of door hinges. Before Mannie could jump up, before Carter could pull himself forward to retrieve the folder waiting naked on the table, Abby stepped into the room.

"Carter?" Her whole body turned. "What are you doing here?"

He reached for the folder, but it was too late. The place was already seething with guilt. Mannie answered for him. "He's helping me with a writing project."

If Carter was trying to hide their work, he was doing a poor job. She was already beside him, taking the papers from his hand. She flipped through them, scanning the notes.

"What is this?" she asked of Mannie.

He coughed. There was no sense lying to the girl. "I asked Carter to stop over . . . to help me write my obituary."

Her eyes squinted. "Why would you want to do that?" she asked, cocking her head to one side.

Mannie made the mistake of trying to be funny. "He seemed like a capable writer, and . . ."

Abby would have none of it. Her chin firmed. Her face flushed. Her neck muscles tensed. "Don't mock me, Mannie. You know what I'm asking. Why are you writing your obituary?"

Mannie released the air he'd been holding in his lungs. He leaned back and motioned for Abby to sit. "I'm sick, honey. I have a . . . a disease that I didn't tell you about."

Abby didn't sit. She took a step closer. "What disease?" she demanded.

"It's called amyloidosis," he said sheepishly, as if that would make the news easier for her to hear. "It's enlarging my heart. Eventually, my organs are going to give out. There's no cure, there's no treatment, there's nothing they can do."

The truth was heavy. Her bottom lip now trembled, shaking with surprise, distress, anger. "How long have you known?"

His timid words begged they not be pushed from his lips. "Since October."

"How long . . . how long do you have?"

"I'm taking some pills that help. . . . They don't know, exactly. Maybe another three or four months."

"Why didn't you tell me?"

"Honey, I didn't want to ruin Christmas for you. I know how much you love the holidays. I was going to tell you right after, I promise."

Her hands joined the quivering. Was it anger or frustration that lifted her voice? "And you didn't think *this* would ruin my Christmas? We don't celebrate Christmas by lying. Never. *Never, Mannie!*"

Her interrogation had focused solely on her uncle. She turned now for the first time to address Carter. "And you've known the entire time?"

Carter's breathing quickened. The answer was rancid and yet he couldn't spit it out. No matter—he was sure she could see the surrendering guilt spilling from his eyes. "And you said nothing to me? *Nothing?*" The nerves in his stomach twisted and tightened.

"How often have you been coming here?" she asked, a question that cuffed him caustically across his face.

Carter held up two fingers. His answer barely choked out. "A couple of times a week, I guess, for a few weeks now."

Resentment gathered into tears. "How could you keep this a secret from me, Carter? How?" It was not her tone that punctured his heart, but rather her disappointment. As her gaze dropped to the floor, his followed. There was a picture on the table that caught her eye. She reached for it, picked it up, studied it.

"Where did you get this?" Her question was directed at Mannie but followed his stare to Carter. She repeated her words with more force, in case he didn't understand. *"I said, where did you get this?"*

"It was in your car . . . at the tow lot. I found it there and I meant to give it back, but I . . ." There was no good way to finish the sentence. Carter's silence sagged under its own weight.

With the picture still clutched in her fingers, her head still shaking, Abby fled from the room the same way she'd entered.

It was Mannie who pried through the disdainful silence she had left behind. "Give her a little time to cool off," he said. "I'll have a talk with her." His attempt to sound confident caught fire and then nosedived.

Carter ignored the advice and instead chased Abby out into the driveway. He reached her as she was climbing into her car.

"Abby, please, give me a chance." Every word begged.

He grasped her hand, which was resting on the handle, but she pulled it away. It was hot to the touch. She turned, faced him, snarled like a threatened animal.

"Carter Cross, if there is one thing in a relationship that's important to me, it's that we can talk about anything. *Anything!* Without that, we have nothing." Surprisingly, her next words fell to a whisper. "My uncle is dying and you knew and you didn't say a word."

She glared at the picture still in her hand. It must have been repulsive to her because she tossed it at Carter's feet. "What other secrets do you have? What else are you hiding?"

"Abby, there's nothing else. I swear!" Panic circled his neck, plunged into his chest.

Her follow-up question was a simple one. "How am I supposed to believe you?" The tremble in her cheeks cued sadness, which she tried to wipe away with shaky fingers. She began to sob softly, but her outstretched arm instructed him to keep his distance. Then, with Carter helplessly watching, she climbed into her car, gently closed the door, and drove off into the night alone.

Chapter 19

Life Set to Music

Yin swerved to the curb at the airport's passenger unloading zone and waited for Carter to gather his luggage.

"Remind me again when you return?" he asked.

"The wedding is tomorrow. I stay with my brother, Grayson, in Spokane through Christmas, then head to Sunnyvale for my meeting on the twenty-eighth. I should be home to wrap things up by New Year's."

Yin turned off the car and tipped back his head. "This all happened so quickly!"

Carter didn't argue. "Life has a funny way of messing with you, that's for certain."

Yin asked hesitantly, "Have you talked to her?"

Carter held the weight of the heavy words. Both

understood that Yin meant Abby. "I left a message on her phone, but she hasn't responded."

"But you'll call her again?" Yin confirmed.

The thought rattled through Carter's head, then lodged in between a cough and a swallow. "You sound like my mother," he said. "I left her a message. I'm not a stalker. If she wants to be in touch, she'll call."

His answer shivered.

He grabbed a breath and his backpack, then lifted his free arm in a half wave toward Yin, his best effort at a parting thank you. He reached toward his obedient suitcase, coaxing it to fall in line behind him. And then, with helplessness still oozing, he wandered away to brave the rushing holiday crowds.

*

As Carter exited the concourse in Seattle, a man of perhaps sixty held a lettered sign displaying Carter's name.

"I think you're waiting for me," Carter told him. But the way the man hesitated, then stepped back for a better look, made it obvious that he was more than a driver.

He lowered the sign, extended his open hand, waited for Carter to shake it. "Carter! I've heard a lot about you. I'm Joel Penton. Your mom is busy with some last-minute wedding details—you know women—so she sent me. I hope that's okay. It's so nice to finally meet you."

Carter would guess Joel was about the same age as Lorella, perhaps a year or two older, and taller, more trim than he had expected from the picture his mother had shown him in Springfield. Today the man wore slacks and a striped button-down shirt, neatly pressed.

"I'm parked in the short-term lot. Are you waiting for luggage?" he asked.

"I've just got my backpack and carry-on," Carter replied.

"We're sure glad you could make it. It means a lot to your mother," Joel said, in a tone that sounded genuine enough, with no hint of condescension. Then he waited for Carter to walk side by side, instead of stepping out in front to lead the way, as Carter's father would have done.

"So what do you do, Joel?" Carter asked, hoping his questions would fill the silence but still sound unassuming.

"I work in finance. I'm the CFO for DigiPlan. We're an electrical engineering firm."

They located his car, a Volvo XC60, and while they drove back to the house, Joel and Carter continued to make small talk: weather, golf, NBA standings, back-packing, and whether two-wheel-drive or all-wheel-drive vehicles were more practical for Seattle's climate. For the half hour they spent together, Carter found the man to be unusually pleasant, even interesting. And for a handful of minutes, he nearly forgot that CFO Joel Penton from Seattle, Washington, who already had several children of his own, would soon be sleeping with Carter's mother.

❄

The wedding was booked at Belle Gardens, a setting that to any bride was a blissful five acres of heaven. Among its most adored features—and most photographed—was a waterfall and pond, complete with a boat so lovers could row a few feet from shore while admiring crowds swooned on the bank, shooting enough Instagram-worthy pictures to clog the Internet for days. The dock was decorated with hundreds of twinkling lights that reminded Carter of the colored light display he and Abby had visited at Forest Park.

In addition, there was a garden encircling an oversized gazebo, adjacent to a Victorian cottage replete with vintage furniture. Even in the winter, the home and grounds were spectacular. Merely add a bride and groom and it completed a scene that would make Norman Rockwell weak in the knees.

Carter listened as "Baby, It's Cold Outside" began

to play romantically in the background. Although he remained uneasy about his mother creating a brand-new life with someone unknown—as nice as the man seemed—the evening simply proved to be the ultimate embellishment. Any wayward situation could be dressed up when it was set to the right music.

When "Santa Baby" cued up next, Carter couldn't help but pull out his phone and check for messages. There were none.

All morning Carter had been helping his scurrying mother finish a few of the final details—placing table centerpieces, hanging roses upside down on strings in the hallway, filling dishes with packaged mints all imprinted with the initials L & J—and frankly, now that the moment had almost arrived, he longed for something more to keep his mind busy.

The ceremony would begin in forty minutes, and already the early arriving overachievers were filtering in through the door. He recognized a few of the faces—Darcel Sims, the neighbor three doors down who always baked banana bread; Mr. Hinning and his wife, who played golf with his parents at the club; and Yvonne Kane, who served with Lorella at the Rotary.

And then, like a shark fin breaking calm water, Carter noticed a gray head of perfectly moussed hair rise up from behind an entering couple. Carter swayed sideways, bending like a willow in the wind as he bowed for a better look.

The man noticed Carter, strode toward him, stopped a foot short, then scanned him from head to toe, as if examining merchandise he was considering for purchase.

Carter wanted to say *Hello,* or *It's been a long time,* or *I have no idea what you're doing here,* but the words huddled in his throat.

The man's eyes drew close and his forehead pleated, as if confused at the hush. When he extended his hand, however, the quiet scattered, accepting the reality that the two could never occupy the same space.

"Hello, Carter," he boomed, loud enough to deafen anyone in a five-foot radius. "I hoped you'd be here!"

Carter took the man's outstretched hand, shook it, and then pointed to a waiting table where they could sit and talk.

"Hi, Dad. How have you been?"

Chapter 20

The Dilemma

Mannie pulled on his old brown slippers, the ones Abby had threatened to throw away because they were separating at the heel, and shuffled out the door toward the mailbox.

He'd been given orders to keep his activity to a minimum, but he was also not supposed to stay bedridden. "Just be careful to not overdo things," the doctor had instructed. Certainly Mannie's daily afternoon trips to get the mail would meet with approval.

A dozen steps away from the house, a pain shot down his left arm to linger in the fingers of his hand. It was a familiar sensation, but one he hadn't noticed since starting the trial drug.

He flexed his fingers, shook at the numbness, hoping it would push out his fingertips to the sidewalk and scurry away. Another six steps and he could feel perspiration mustering across his brow.

He reached the mailbox, pulled open the lid, and found only a flyer from a local carpet cleaning service, a credit card offer, and a bill from the gas company. Clenching all three in his right hand, he prepared to trek back to the house with a promise to lie down until the symptoms passed.

Perhaps later in the afternoon, he would even try calling Abby again to see if she was ready to come over and talk. He wanted to thoroughly explain the situation with Carter, confess that it was all her crazy uncle's fault, clarify that it was he who had insisted the boy keep everything a secret. He needed to convince her that she and Carter should patch things up and get back together—because he genuinely liked Carter.

As Mannie pivoted, a pain exploded in his chest that felt like an angry lion clawing apart his heart. The mail in his hands dropped to the cement and scattered. He tried to suck in air, but it only fanned the firestorm unfurling in his ribcage.

He recognized that it must be a heart attack, but prayed it wouldn't be the end. He reached into his pocket for his phone to call for help, but it was not there. He'd left it on the kitchen table.

His breaths were shallow—too shallow—and by not drawing enough oxygen into his lungs, he understood that he would soon pass out.

He dropped to the curb, half sitting, half falling, and despite the lack of a phone, his lips began calling, speaking words meant for only one to hear.

"Please, not until after Christmas. Not yet. Please, not un—"

Before he could finish his plea a second time, the sky turned a punishing black, the noises around him closed their mouths, and Mannie Foster McBride slumped motionless onto the cold and unforgiving December ground.

Burnell Cross, Carter's father, was a smartly dressed man with a stout nose, styled hair, and a pragmatic stare—a man who pushed middle age to its limits. He was wearing a suit that cost more than a penthouse mortgage payment and shoes that spoke fluent Italian.

Carter positioned himself beside the man, let his jaw lower, but then seemingly paused to rest. "Do you have something to say?" Burnell finally asked.

"I guess I'm still trying to process that you're here."

Burnell's bushy gray eyebrows lifted. "Your mom's getting married. Why wouldn't I be here?"

It was a fumbled pause, the kind that gropes for lost words. When the words arrived, they carried confusion. "Exactly my point. Since you and mom split up . . . and considering that she's marrying another man . . . I thought that you'd be . . . *angry*."

Burnell bent in with a smile that was close to coy, as if he were sharing inside information at the horse track. "I admit, I do hate to lose—but at least it's not a court case!"

He appeared to wait for a laugh, but it was a tough crowd. Carter winced instead. "So you truly don't care?"

Burnell leaned back, his words leaning with him. "I didn't say that. Look, Carter, we married young. We made mistakes." Without any prodding, he corrected himself. "*I* made mistakes. I'm not expecting to collect a trophy. At this point, I just hope she's happy—and I think she will be. Joel can provide things I can't."

"You call him *Joel?*" The question flinched.

"Why?" His father's eyes narrowed. "What do you call him?"

Carter's silence shrugged.

Burnell continued, "Honestly, he seems like a decent

178

guy. How can I be anything but pleased for both of them? Besides, her marriage reduces my alimony."

Again, with no hint of amusement leaking from Carter, only a pregnant pause, Burnell changed the subject. "So your mom told me about your job offer. I'm proud of you. I have to admit, when you turned down law school and moved away, I didn't expect you'd make much of your life."

"That's a compliment, right?" Carter replied dryly. "Because I'm getting all warm and fuzzy."

"You know me. I say it like I see it—and I'm telling you, you're doing okay. I'm proud of you."

The words fell to the ground and waited. Carter wasn't sure how to pick them up. But, for the first time since their conversation had begun, the tension gripping Carter's shoulders slackened.

"Can I ask you something?" Carter finally said. "You know, get some fatherly advice?"

"As you've learned by now, it's not my specialty," Burnell replied. "But I can give you an expert legal opinion."

Carter's sigh conceded. "At this point, I think I'll take it."

Burnell straightened. "Perfect," he said, now on the clock. "What's the problem?"

The words were ready, even anxious. "There's a girl I've been dating, Abby, who lives in Springfield. She runs a store there with her uncle, but he's sick. If I take the job in California, I'll be walking away from the relationship, and I don't want to do that. On the other hand, the job offer is totally amazing. We're talking six figures, an expense account, a career I would love. So you see, it's a dilemma. I truthfully don't know what to do."

Burnell's fingers intertwined. He rested them noticeably against his chin, as if it helped him think. "It seems pretty straightforward to me," he finally said.

"It does?"

"Sure, this is a case of *value in use* versus *value in exchange.*"

Carter's head listed to one side. "I don't know what that means."

Burnell was speaking low, as if a jury were listening. "They're legal terms," he offered. "*Value in use* weighs the utility of an object in satisfying—directly or indirectly—the needs or desires of human beings. *Value in exchange* represents the cost in an open market to replace said commodity—in this case, the girl. It's simple, really. Make your decision as to the best valuation method. If it's *value in exchange,* for example, then compare the acquisition value—I'm talking the cost for a similar girl in Sunnyvale—to what you'd be giving up to forego the job, and I think it will all become pretty clear. As for me, from experience, I would suggest *value in use.*"

"Acquisition of a similar girl in Sunnyvale?" Carter echoed. His open mouth made a perfect circle. He expected a hint of sarcasm, but there was no smirk, no sneer, no turn of his father's frown. The man had never been more serious.

"The numbers don't lie," Burnell added, as if no one could now argue. "I should know. You won't go wrong with *value in use.*"

The flowing wisdom was interrupted by "Santa Baby" crooning from Carter's pocket. His cell phone was ringing.

❋

"Abby?"

"No, Carter, it's Seven." Her words were restless, fearful.

"Seven? What's wrong?"

They either had a bad connection or she was gathering her thoughts. "Mannie's had a heart attack. Abby's not sure if he's going to make it. A neighbor found him in the street, out by his mailbox. He was unconscious, barely breathing. We're at the hospital with him now. I wanted you to be aware."

Angst anchored itself to Carter and began to pull him under.

"Seven, I'm in Seattle." It wasn't an excuse, simply a fact.

"I understand."

Anxiety latched onto every word. "Should I try to fly back? Would it help?"

"You'll need to decide." He heard her voice wobble. "I just thought you should know."

❄

Carter found his mother lined up ready for the procession music to begin. White dress notwithstanding, the moment she looked into Carter's face, she knew something was wrong.

"What is it?" she asked, taking his hands.

His words came out as a tremble. "I got a call. Abby's uncle's had a heart attack." There was no easy way to break the news. "Mom, I have to go!"

Lorella motioned to one of the waiting flower girls.

"Susan, dear, run quick and get your uncle Joel. Tell him to hurry!"

When the child returned, she was tugging more than Joel. Seeing the commotion, Burnell had joined in and was bringing up the rear.

"What is it?" Joel asked, wearing all the terror of a cancelled wedding.

Lorella filled him in. "It's an emergency. Abby's father—Abby is Carter's girlfriend—he's had a heart attack. Carter has to leave!"

"Can't it wait until after the wedding?" Burnell asked with unintended brashness.

Lorella left no room for debate. "No!" she retorted. "He needs to go now! If he misses the last flight he'll have to wait until morning and . . . well, that won't do."

"Have you called the airlines?" Joel wondered. He didn't wait for an answer to explain. "My friend works for the airport authority. He can pull some strings. Let me find out if he's working." Joel clutched his phone and dialed.

Carter rocked forward on his toes. The ceremony was supposed to be starting, and he was holding it up for everyone. "Mom, I'm completely messing up your wedding. I feel terrible. I'll just wait!"

"*Carter James Cross!*" No one misunderstood her tone. "Do you love this girl or don't you?"

Nobody had ever asked him so directly, so forcefully. He didn't need to wrestle with the words. "Yes . . . yes, I do!"

"Then look around, Son. Learn something. Don't be sorry later."

It was Burnell's turn to weight-shift. He seemed to sense he was part of her lesson, but he didn't disagree. "I told you," he reinforced, with a slap to Carter's back. "*Value in use.* It's the one I should have used."

Carter's eyes must have been scrunching. "I'll explain it again to you later," his father said, "and I want you to listen more carefully next time."

Joel was barely hanging up his phone. "Evan is working," he confirmed. "He'll meet you at the curb. If there's any chance of you flying out tonight, you need to leave now!"

"Let me call a cab," Carter said.

"There's no time," Joel replied. "Lorella, can we delay the wedding an hour? I'll take him."

Carter spun a quarter turn. He was facing both Joel and Lorella. "No, no, no! You're getting married!" he hollered, since it appeared the crazies had suddenly forgotten the purpose of their own gathering.

"I can take him." The voice belonged to Grayson, Carter's older brother, who must have wandered up from behind.

Silence confirmed that the family finally agreed on something.

"We'll still delay an hour," Lorella told him. "Can you be back?"

"I'll do my best," Grayson replied. He turned to direct Carter. "I'll pull up the car and meet you out front."

As Grayson trotted away, Carter reached across to embrace his mother. His words were coated with candor. "I'm sorry to have come this far and then miss your wedding. I'm also sorry I was so weirded out by all of this at first. I can see that Joel really is a terrific guy, and I'm extremely happy for you."

"That's all that I wanted you to see, so thank you!" The twinkle in her eyes was as bright as the surrounding Christmas lights. "And simply because we're a bit dysfunctional," she added, "doesn't mean we aren't always here for you."

He hugged her and perhaps held her too tight because when he pulled away she was trickling tears.

"And bring Abby with you next time," she sniffled. Then she glimpsed her watch. Her tears instantly scattered as her voice assumed a level closer to Burnell's. "*Now, go!*" she commanded.

Carter mouthed his last thank you, turned toward the entrance . . . and ran.

Chapter 21

The Plea

Grayson Cross was three years older than Carter—and three years more intimidating. In high school, he'd lettered in basketball, dated a cheerleader, made the honor roll. Grayson, unlike the wayward second child in the family, had followed in his father's footsteps to Cornell, graduated with honors, then taken an associate position at his father's firm. There was no question he was the preferred son; when Carter was still living at home, friends and neighbors commonly referred to Carter as *Grayson's brother.*

"I appreciate the ride to the airport," Carter told him for the umpteenth time.

"Relax," replied Grayson. "As I said, it's no problem."

For the next minute no words were spoken, and what

should have been comfortable silence between brothers swelled into awkwardness. Carter used a question to cut the apprehension.

"Can I ask you something?"

"Sure."

"Do you know what *value in use* means?"

Grayson laughed low and long, giving both of them time to relax. "Don't tell me that Dad gave you the *value in use* lecture?"

"Then you've heard it?"

"Sure. He mentions it a lot, especially when he's drunk. I'm curious . . . did the context have something to do with a girl?"

"How did you know? What does it mean?"

"It's Dad's way of admitting that he blew it."

"I'm not sure I follow."

"Let me see if I can get his definition right. Value in use weighs the utility of an object in satisfying—directly or indirectly—the needs or desires of human beings. Does that sound about right?"

"That's it exactly."

"It's the value of something you can't put a price on. The *desire of human beings* is, of course, love. It's Dad's way of conceding that relationships rather than money may in fact be what makes life worth living."

"*Our* dad?" Carter questioned.

"He has his moments," Grayson replied, his gaze calm and kind. "Granted, they're few and far between—and, as I said, sometimes liquor is involved."

Carter shook his head, dusted away the doubt. "How about you? How is life at the firm? Have you made partner yet?"

Grayson's smirk uncurled. It was a look that said he couldn't tell if Carter was being serious or not. "Now you're just mocking me, aren't you?"

Wrinkles folded at the corners of Carter's eyes. "Mocking you? What are you talking about?"

Grayson glanced from the road to Carter. "You're rubbing it in that I'm stuck at the firm and you're not."

Every muscle in Carter's face read he was clueless. "I'm completely serious. You're an attorney. You're making a killing. You own a home. You're following your dream. Me? I'm technically unemployed at the moment. At least one of us is making Dad proud."

Grayson's grin returned, but the corners were weighted down with disbelief. "You're so dense sometimes it's laughable," he told him. "Dad pressured us both to go to law school, and I was too timid to stand up to him. You, on the other hand, had the sense to walk away, to get out. You don't even see that, do you?" He gestured toward Carter with his nose, as if trained to sniff out the foolhardy.

"I've never looked at it that way," Carter said. "I guess I always considered myself the disappointment."

"Whether Dad appreciates it or not, I'm telling you that I admire what you did. It took courage. Going to law school, following Dad's footsteps—that was the easy way out, and easy always comes at a price."

Carter let the thought swim around him before pivoting the topic. "What do you think of Joel?"

"As far as I can tell, he and Mom are pretty great together. I'm kind of happy for them both. You?"

This time Carter's reply was soft around the edges. "Joel seems . . . fabulous. Grayson?"

"Yes?"

"Next time I come out, which will be soon, I'd love for us to spend some time together, go golfing, genuinely catch up. What do you say?"

The silence was finally warm.

"I can't wait."

When Joel said his friend had connections, he wasn't joking. Evan was waiting as Carter arrived at the airport.

He ushered Carter into a nearby office suite and then slid behind a computer. He tapped the keyboard like a seasoned secretary.

"Here's what we've got. Unfortunately, you've missed the last flight leaving for Hartford tonight. You can stay overnight here—I can get you a room at the Hilton next to the airport and then get you on a flight first thing in the morning . . ." he hit a few more keys " . . . that will get you there tomorrow night, around nine." More tapping, more scribbling codes on a piece of scratch paper with his pen, "Or . . . there's a redeye that leaves in an hour that will get you into Boston by morning. You can grab a rental car and be in Springfield by noon." He glanced to Carter for his preference.

"Boston sounds like the better choice, right?"

"There's one issue," the man added, twisting the screen around for Carter to see. "I can see the weather warnings sent to the pilots, and it appears there's a storm blowing down the coast that they have a close eye on. They've flagged it as a potential divert or delay, which could happen before you land in Boston. It's unlikely but possible. I'll let you make the call."

"I'm still thinking Boston," Carter said, watching to see if the man agreed. As an afterthought, Carter asked, "What's the price difference between the two flights?"

The man's scrunching eyebrows deflected all concern. "I spoke with Joel, and we've got this covered for you."

Carter offered a gracious nod, considered, calculated, and then concluded. He turned to the man waiting behind the computer.

"Send me to Boston!"

❅

With just twenty minutes until he was to board his flight, Carter dialed his mother. He told her to thank Joel, then listened to her recite how grateful she was that he had come out. He could hear the wedding party raging in the background and had to threaten to hang up to convince her to return to her guests.

Carter had one more call to make.

His dad's phone clicked right to voice mail. Carter considered calling back but decided if he didn't get the words out now, they may refuse later.

"Dad, this is Carter. I've been thinking about the situation between you and Mom—the divorce and her new marriage—and . . . I blamed you. I realize now that it wasn't my place, and I'm sorry. Please forgive me. Plus, I sincerely appreciate your advice on *value in use.* I've been thinking about the concept and I plan to take it to heart."

He paused for a second, waiting for the words to catch up with his thoughts. "Next time I come out, I'm going to bring Abby. I'd like you to meet her." It was a notion that carted contentment. "I'm boarding now, so I'll call you later. Thanks, Dad."

※

Abby tilted forward to keep her legs from falling asleep. The chair, though hospital worthy, was about as comfortable as raw plywood—but she wouldn't leave. She held Mannie's fingers, occasionally squeezing, continually praying he would soon squeeze back.

The door cracked open, and Seven slid into the room.

"Abby, let me sit with him for a while. You go home and get some sleep."

Abby squinted her confusion. "I thought you were taking Rosa and André home."

"Honey, I did. Now I'm back to spell you off."

Seven had already edged against the bed, already rested her hand on Mannie's. She was not giving Abby a choice.

"I can't go home," Abby contested. "I wouldn't sleep there, either, and at least here I'm not alone."

Seven's head lifted and then lowered. It was as if

she expected nothing less. "Then at least let me sit with Mannie while you go and get something to eat. It's been hours, and I insist."

Abby's eyes shone gratitude. Not for the chance to eat, but for knowing that there were others around who truly cared.

"I'll be right back," she whispered.

She freed Seven's hand, shuffled zombielike to the cafeteria—surprised to find it still open—and bought a plastic-bowled salad she likely wouldn't eat. She sat at a table near the window and subconsciously segregated the bowl's contents with her fork.

The words she'd been repeating to Mannie clung to her, still reeking of despair. "Don't leave me, Uncle. I'm not ready to have you go. I'm not ready to face life alone."

The cafeteria sat on the ground floor, and as she glanced at the outside window, a misty image of the moon filled the pane. She was too young to remember her parents' passing, but she'd been told the story of how she watched the moon from an adjacent room as those closest to her quietly slipped away.

Tonight, the eerie moonlight filled her with panic, representing only sorrow and death. She stood, left her uneaten salad on the table, and hurried back to be with Mannie.

Two doors away, she passed another room with a window to the outside world, this one covered with stained glass. It was the hospital chapel, and, despite her anxiety, she couldn't help but step inside.

At this late hour, she was alone, and her intent was to hurry to the front, bow silently in a pew beside the stained-glass image of Christ, and offer a quick but heartfelt prayer. Then a twinkle of light near the opposite wall snared her attention. It was a makeshift manger scene, lit with strands of white Christmas lights, and it drew her close like the smell of baking cookies might draw a child.

She was looking for a spot to pray, and it would do fine.

As she waited for the words to assemble, irony also edged in through the colored glass. The moonlight illuminated the makeshift cradle, highlighting the obvious message: People come into the world and people go. Birth and death hold hands. It's the way life has been for a million years.

The truth of it didn't stop her heart from aching. *Is there a heavenly allocation,* she wondered? *Do we all have our appointed time to die, or does heaven offer some flexibility in the process?*

As she contemplated death and birth, a thought she knew to be selfish squirmed into her head. It was an idea that became a whispered plea. "I get that dying is an inevitable part of life, that every day babies are born and people pass—but I need more time. If there's some sort of quota, some universal balance in play, I'm asking if there's somebody else you can take tonight, someone who can step in instead? God, I can't lose Mannie at Christmas. I simply can't."

No sooner had she let the words go than she wished she could gather them back. "I'm sorry," she said, shaking her head in disgust toward the manger. "That was a terrible and self-centered thing for me to say."

But the words were already floating through the tinted window, winding their way heavenward. And, as many answered prayers will attest, sometimes uttered words are impossible to take back.

Abby quietly left the chapel and walked back to Mannie's room. When she pulled open the door, her heart sank. Seven was seated in the chair beside the bed with tears channeling down both her cheeks. She was watching a doctor and nurse, one on each side of the bed, work on Mannie.

"No!" Abby screamed as she bolted toward them, but Seven jumped up to stop her midstep. "Abby, don't worry," she said smiling, almost laughing. "These are happy tears! Mannie squeezed my hand!"

＊

Just a few hours later, Mannie was sitting up. He was awake and still tethered to the incessantly beeping monitor, but he was complaining about it, so it was a positive sign. The doctor came in, seemed surprised at how well his patient was recovering, then explained that they would continue to run tests, that Mannie's heart was still enlarged, that the disease hadn't gone away. He said that although Mannie had indeed suffered a mild myocardial infarction, it was likely the lack of oxygen triggered by Mannie's condition that had caused him to lose consciousness. And there were some remedies to address that.

Abby gripped Mannie's fingers, squeezed her appreciation, could still scarcely believe the turn of events. "I couldn't have you go at Christmas," she repeated, as if his improvement were her doing.

"I'm not going anywhere," Mannie replied. "At least, not yet." And then he passed her a look that let her know it was time they talked.

"We can chat later," Abby told him. "You need to rest now."

"You need to listen," he said, "since in truth neither one of us knows how much 'later' I have left in me."

She recognized that arguing would only agitate him

further, so she scooted in close and gave Mannie her full attention.

"Have you talked to Carter?" he asked.

She shook her head. "I tried to call but it went directly to voice mail."

"There's something I need to tell you. I know you're angry that he didn't say anything to you about me being sick, and you think that means you can't trust him." Abby didn't move, didn't voice her agreement. She just listened. "But I'm telling you now that Carter not telling you about me means he's probably the most trustworthy person you'll ever meet."

Abby weighed Mannie's words, doing her best to reconcile them. "What do you mean?"

"Listen. I made Carter swear that he wouldn't tell you. He was keeping a promise to me, an ornery old fart he hardly knew, when every other guy in the world would have spilled his guts in ten seconds to the beautiful girl. No, Abby, Carter may have many faults, but I'm telling you here and now that not being trustworthy most certainly isn't one of them."

If she harbored any lingering doubt about Carter, it cowered at Mannie's explanation—and the man wasn't finished. "You also need to know that he cares for you. I could see it the moment I saw you two walk in the room together on that first day. The way he looked at you—you can't fake that, and you can't hide it."

As Abby listened, a lump rose in her throat. It tasted an awful lot like the truth.

"I know you weren't as smitten at first," he continued. "I could tell that as well. But I've seen an affection grow in your eyes since. I think you care for him, too."

If he meant to make her tear up, then mission accomplished.

"What should I do, Uncle?" she asked. "I should call him again, shouldn't I?" She pulled out her phone, pressed in his number, waited for it to ring, but it switched instantly to voice mail.

"Hello, this is Carter. Leave a message and I'll call you back as soon as I'm able."

Chapter 22

The Playlist

Carter's plane landed in Boston, but barely. The weather report was dead-on, meaning the ride was bumpy, his flight was late, and the prognosticator deserved a gold star for his forehead. As Carter made his way to the rental-car counter, he heard a worker mention that the runways were being shut down. It meant he had made it in the nick of time.

Joel had called ahead, already made a reservation, and covered the charges, so the woman behind the counter had just one question: "What size car would you like?"

Carter was about to tell her that it didn't matter, that he was alone and had just the single bag and his backpack. Then a thought struck. "Do you by chance have a Ford Fiesta?"

Her brow wrinkled and her lips drew back, as if perhaps it was the first time said words had ever been uttered at the company. "No, no, sorry. No Fiestas in the rental pool here. Anything else?"

Carter was thinking about Abby's playlist. It seemed fitting. He pulled out his phone, held it up for the attendant to see. "Do you have a car with a Bluetooth connection, so I can listen to music on my phone?"

Her head nodded. "*That* we can do!"

And in only a matter of minutes, Carter had signed the papers, located the car, tossed his suitcase in the back, unzipped it to retrieve his gloves, and climbed into the front seat. The snow was coming down fiercely, and he had no time to lose. But before he pulled the car into gear, he set his phone on the passenger's seat and synced it to the car's sound system.

The drive would be miserable, the roads treacherous; the storm had made certain of that. Carter didn't care. He turned up the heat, turned up the volume, turned up the corners of his mouth. He would do it for Abby. He'd drive back through the snow, singing along to her favorite music on the stereo. He would make the best of it, even if he had to pretend.

After all, it was almost Christmas.

While the words to "Winter Wonderland" almost frolicked out of the car's inside speakers, outside it was anything but wonderful. The storm was showing its contempt, furious that anyone would dare to drive through it.

There was traffic on the turnpike coming out of Boston, naturally, but the farther away Carter drove from the city, the more it thinned. By the time he passed Auburn, only the dim or the desperate were still trying to navigate the roads.

Carter passed two snowplows as he headed toward Charlton, but they looked exhausted, as the snow was coming down faster than it could be cleared. He wasn't worried. Despite the wipers working overtime to keep the windshield clean, the car was navigating well. At his current pace, he would arrive within the hour.

Carter reached to the passenger's seat for his phone and tried to dial Abby. However, it barely showed a single bar—perhaps due to the storm—and the call dropped before it connected. He would try again later. Next, he fished for his charging cable. The phone had been feeding Abby's Christmas songs into the stereo since he had left the airport, and he needed to plug it in to recharge the battery. He found the end, pushed the cable into the phone and connected it securely, then rested it again on the seat beside him. However, when his gaze lifted back to the road, two deer were standing broadside in the turnpike. The closest had his head twisted toward the car, as if he couldn't figure out why headlights would be barreling through the snow at such a high rate of speed.

Carter lifted his foot, readied to slam the brakes, but it was too late. Metal crunched, deer bones shattered, the airbag violently exploded. The car flipped sideways, hurtled toward the guardrail, then smashed into the rail on the driver's side. Carter's head cracked against the window, and glass shattered.

Perhaps it was the snow, perhaps it was the angle of the car due to its impact with the deer, perhaps it was pure chance, but as the car hit the railing, it tipped, slid, then rolled over it like a toy tossed aside by an angry child.

It somersaulted once, twice, and then half again as it tumbled down the embankment—*bam, bam, bam*—cold metal colliding each quarter turn against snow, earth, and rock, until it rested lifeless and upside down at the bottom.

Carter's eyes were closed. He was breathing, but not moving.

Blood trickled from a cut on the side of his head—*drip, drip, drip*—to mix with snow that was blowing in through the broken window to settle on the inside car roof below Carter's head.

Abby had told Carter that a fresh blanket of snow made even the ugliest of scenes more beautiful, and it was true. Within a few minutes, someone could have stood on the road where the car had plunged over the guardrail, glanced out across the scene, noticed nothing but magical beauty, and declared, "*It's the most wonderful time of the year.*"

When Carter woke, he was cold, his head was pounding, he could taste blood, and he was strapped upside down in an overturned car. He wasn't certain how long he'd been out, and although it was still light outside, it felt like it could be dusk. He tried to wriggle free, but he couldn't move his legs.

He reached for the seat belt and was about to unfasten

it, but the steering column had been pushed toward the seat, tightly pinning his calves underneath. Until he could get his legs free, he would need the support of the lap and shoulder belts to keep him from twisting upside down by injured limbs.

He tried to move his feet, found that he could wiggle them, and took it as a sign that his legs and ankles were not broken. His head was bleeding, so he looked for something to hold against the wound. He glanced down toward the ground, which was now the inside roof, to see a jumble of clothes, papers, shoes, snow, and glass. His suitcase had been unzipped on the backseat, so when the car had repeatedly flipped, its contents had been properly churned before settling in a strewn layer below him. He reached up, which was actually down, grasped for a T-shirt, and pressed it against his head. It spotted with blood, but the wound didn't seem to be spurting, and so, he reasoned, he just needed to stay calm and think.

He tried again to free his legs but couldn't stop his claim-adjuster instincts from also tabulating the vehicle damage. Considering the distance the steering column had traveled, the engine's displacement, and the structural frame damage, this car would likely be totaled.

"Breathe," he commanded aloud, once he realized what he was doing. "Relax! Help will be coming."

But would it? It was still snowing, and there had been no cars on the road behind him. It was likely no one saw the accident, but would they see the tire tracks? Carter peered out the hole once covered by the window, an opening where flakes were now blowing in as if they wanted to inspect the accident, see what was inside. Any tire imprints veering off the road would soon be covered, if they hadn't been already. The snow had done a stellar job of hiding anything unsightly or unclean.

Then Carter remembered the deer. Would someone see the dead animal and stop to investigate? If so, wouldn't they assume the damaged car had kept driving? What would lead them to hike over the embankment? The answer chilled every muscle.

Nothing!

Carter pushed the horn, hoping someone would hear it from the roadway. It must have been damaged because, in place of a blasting trumpet, the sound was closer to that of someone pillow-smothering a duck.

Think! Think!

Carter again considered the dead deer, only this time a grin followed, perhaps unintended levity stemming from an oversupply of blood pumping to his upside-down head. He was remembering the moment before impact and wishing desperately someone else were there so he could explain the irony: Just before he had slammed broadside into the helpless creature, the song playing from Abby's list—which was wide and eclectic—was Chuck Berry's "Run Rudolph Run."

Rudolph should have listened.

Wait, Carter thought, *my phone!* He reached again into the mess below him, brushed papers aside, and frantically craned his neck. He pulled at his legs to stretch farther, but the pain reeled him back.

There was no phone in sight.

Perhaps it didn't matter. With the storm disrupting the service, what good would it do him anyway?

One more time he attempted to twist his legs free. To no avail—they may as well have been cemented in place. He felt woozy, worried about vomiting, and instead closed his eyes to rest.

He'd never been in an accident, and for the second time in a few minutes, he laughed at himself—an accident adjuster with no clue. They should make having a major accident a requirement for adjusters, he decided, so they would better understand what people experience.

He was embarrassed now that he had had the nerve to ask Abby if she'd smiled right before her accident.

Abby.

The thought of her both soothed and distressed.

What if he never saw her again? He screamed away the thought. "*Help! Anyone, please help!*"

He stopped, listened, waited for someone to answer.

There was no response, nothing but the uncaring silence of falling snow.

❄

Abby was pacing tracks into the hospital carpet. "Seven, I'm nervous!"

She was stating the obvious, and Seven couldn't argue. Abby had called Carter's mother, found out when his flight had landed, talked to the car-rental company, and confirmed he had driven away that morning toward home.

"He should be here by now," Abby added. "He should have been here long ago." They were words she'd been persistently repeating for the last couple of hours.

"Try his phone again," Seven encouraged.

Abby slumped into a chair in the hall outside Mannie's room. She dialed, listened, cringed. "It barely rings, then goes straight to voice mail. That means his phone is off or he doesn't have service, right?"

Seven could only shake her head, lift her shoulders.

Abby bit at her lip. She hadn't told Seven or anyone

about her whispered prayer when she thought Mannie was dying, about wishing for another to step in to take his place. First of all, she didn't mean it. Second, if she did, even a little bit, she certainly didn't intend it to be someone she knew, someone she cared about. It was a stupid thing to worry about anyway. Heaven didn't work that way, did it?

"It's getting dark," she said. "If he's out there, if he's lost . . . Seven, what am I going to do?" Before Seven responded, Abby made a decision. "I'll be back," she told her friend. "I need to run to the bathroom."

It was a lie. Instead, she headed toward the hospital chapel to explain again beside the manger that she was deeply sorry for even thinking such a terrible thing. On the way, she changed her mind. She walked instead to the hospital cafeteria, filled a glass with water, and then took a seat in a booth by the oversized window where she could plainly see the waning moon.

At the moment, she was too ashamed to talk with God. She had another person in mind—her mother.

❄

Carter didn't remember drifting off to sleep, but he must have, because when he woke, it was dark. His vision was blurred, his head felt like fire, and he could hardly move his fingers in the cold. The falling snow had stopped, and the clouds must have cleared because the slightest hint of moonlight crawled into the car to rest beside him. It also meant that as the winter night set in, the temperatures would plummet. He was wearing only a light shirt and would be kidding himself if he thought he could make it until morning.

In the muted light, Carter made out the scattered pages of his Christmas story. The car was littered with them. His manuscript had been sitting inside his un-zipped suitcase. He'd brought a hard copy along to read over in case the wedding turned out to be a total disaster.

It was now rather ironic. He was going to die right before Christmas, in the snow, surrounded by the pages of his own tragic Christmas tale. It confirmed something Abby had once patiently explained as he sat beside her at the bookstore. "In a good story," she had said, "*the ending often circles back to the beginning. Life does that.*" Those were the words she had used, and now they proved true.

But there was tragedy stitched in her lesson. Had it not been for the first accident, he would never have met Abby. Now, because of the second, he would never see her again. How should he reconcile that? It was almost as if heaven were whispering that despite the calamity, *there were no accidents.*

In nearly every Christmas book Carter had read, there was someone close to death, someone begging for a Christmas miracle. If he believed the stories, then this would be the moment that a Christmas ghost of some flavor—past, present, future—would appear by his side and walk him through the reasons he should be grateful for the wonders of his life and for the season.

Carter waited.

Nothing. No ghost. No angel. No miracle.

Oddly, he was consigned to the outcome. If every story were to end miraculously and happily, it would negate the need for hope. That was another writing lesson learned from Abby, a lesson that likewise applied to life. The wonder isn't in the miraculous ending, it's in a changed heart. He tried now to recall her exact words. *Anyone can believe when it's raining miracles. The question is, do we have the strength to believe during the drought?* Then she'd squeezed his hand, kissed him on the cheek, and told him it didn't matter because, as she'd put it, "Christmas *is* the miracle."

Carter's regret was that he wouldn't have a chance to tell her that she'd made a difference, that he was better because of her. She had tried to tell him that Christmas was a choice, but he was hesitant, too skeptical to listen. If she were now sitting beside him, if he could speak to her one last time, he would take her hand, look into her warm eyes, and tell her that he'd also decided to choose Christmas.

He let out a cold breath.

If he could speak to her again, he would tell her that he loved her.

His thoughts were interrupted by music. It took him a minute to recognize the song. It was coming from the backseat, but the tune was unmistakable.

"Santa Baby" was playing from his cell phone.

Abby was calling!

※

One ring. Two rings. Three rings.

"Seven!" Abby screamed. "Finally, it's ringing! It's not going to voice mail!" She stood from her chair. Seven inched close. Mannie looked up.

Four rings. Five rings. Six rings. "Hello, this is Carter Cross. I can't take your call right now, but please leave a message and I'll call you right back."

"It did go to voice mail after all," Abby told the room,

"but after a bunch of rings. What does that mean? What should I do?"

Mannie and Seven answered in unison. "Try again!"

Carter rubbed the cold from his face, twisted his head until his neck burned, squinted his eyes, and ordered them to focus. He couldn't see the phone itself, but in the mess of things scattered across the backseat roof, he could make out a faint glow.

The song ended, rested, then started to play again.

He knew that the phone was well out of reach and was surprised that its battery was not yet dead. Even more startling was that it was connecting. It must have been the clearing sky that was finally letting the signal through.

If only he had a stick or something he could use to reach it . . . but he knew that it was an empty wish. When the ringtone started for the third time, Carter cringed. He ground his teeth. "Santa Baby" was mocking him. It was a beautiful song when it meant he could speak with Abby. It was ugly when it taunted him with the fact that he would never see her again.

The thought wormed into his brain—*ugly, ugly, ugly.*

What was the lesson Abby had loved from his

photography? To find purpose in our problems, to see past the ugliness, rather than step back, we should get closer. Only then will we notice the beauty.

It took but a second for the words to bud. Even the cold couldn't stop them. Carter flexed his freezing fingers. It was an idea that could work. The real question was, were the electronics damaged in the crash?

He would know soon enough.

A moment before, Carter had been praying for the rings to stop. Now he prayed that she wouldn't give up, that she'd try one last time.

The car brimmed with silence, fear, silence.

"Please, Abby. Once more."

The stillness stretched until it felt like hope would break. Then, like angels from heaven, the phone once again began to sing.

Carter's hands trembled—perhaps it was the cold, perhaps it was nerves. He reached toward the ignition. The car wouldn't start—he knew that already from trying earlier, hoping he could run the heater. It was understandable, since the car was upside down.

At the moment, however, he didn't need the car to turn over. He simply needed to turn the key and pray. He twisted the ignition, and the lights flickered. He pleaded that the Bluetooth used to play Abby's songs over the radio would once again automatically connect with his phone.

He rested his finger against the green button on the steering wheel labeled with an icon of an ear. On the third ring, he whispered his prayer and pressed it tightly.

The ringing stopped. The car speakers crackled.

He heard a voice.

"Hello? Carter? Are you there?"

Chapter 23

O Holy Night

One ring, two rings, three rings . . . only this time there was a click, a connection, and static.

"Hello? Carter?" Abby said. "Are you there?" The line crackled. "Carter, where are you?" She raised her volume. "Can you hear me?" Her eyes flooded.

Then she heard him cough. She listened to him rustle. Finally, he spoke. "Abby?" His voice was distant, weak.

"Carter, I'm here! Where are you? What's happened?"

More coughing. More static. His words slurred, and she struggled to stitch the syllables together.

"Carter, I can't hear you very well. Can you repeat that? I can't understand!"

He choked out the plea again, but the sounds broke into nonsensical noise—a piece here, a word there. Then the connection dropped, the line went dead, and hope fell to the cold hospital tile and shattered.

Abby frantically redialed, waited for the line to connect, slumped when it clicked immediately over to voice mail.

"What did he say?" Seven asked. "Could you understand anything?"

Abby's hands shook. She answered Seven as she dialed Carter again. "It was hard to make out what he was saying," she said, "but I think he said that he loves me, but then . . ." Her face glowed with worry.

"Abby, what is it?"

She was trying to make sense, trying to glue his meaning together. "Seven, he said he wanted me to know that he chooses Christmas."

❆

Carter could no longer bend his fingers. He'd finally stopped shivering, but he knew that was not a positive sign. He pushed the horn one last time, but the duck was dead. He waited for his phone, but it no longer rang.

He would have cried, but the cold would allow no more tears.

Mannie had asked Carter for help writing his obituary. Carter's final regret was that he didn't get to write his own.

How will I be remembered?

Before he had met Abby, the answer was easy: *Carter Cross was a man who realized that Christmas is too commercial, that people's motivations are often not pure. He died alone, with an empty heart, but sure in the knowledge that he was right.*

But those words were no longer true. Since he had met Abby, his life had changed. His sleepy lips now barely moved, scarcely mouthed the message he longed to leave: *Carter Cross was a man who discovered hope, who learned that belief can be a choice. While it's true that he died alone—because at times that's how life turns out—he also died content, a Christmas convert, thanks to Abby McBride.*

And let it be known that just before he died, Carter Cross smiled.

In Carter's dream there was a distant white light. Someone was softly calling out his name.

"Carter Cross! Carter Cross!"

The light grew brighter, hotter. His name got louder.

"I see him! He's over here!"

There was a gruff man shouting directions. He was wearing a uniform and a badge that read *Massachusetts Highway Patrol.* "Get the blankets out of my car! We've got to get him warmed up!"

Carter heard sirens and voices and a sound like a lawn mower running beside his ear. There was metal crunching, glass breaking—and the sensation of being carried away.

He woke up enough in the ambulance to realize what was happening and asked how they had been able to find him. The attendant said they had tracked the signal from his phone, then told him to rest, that he needed his strength.

Carter closed his eyes, swearing that in the distant reaches of his head, he could still hear the soft ringing of "Santa Baby."

❄

Carter was taken to Harrington Hospital, where doctors found him to be in surprisingly good shape. His legs were bruised but not broken. The frostbite on his fingers was largely superficial. The laceration on his head was minor. They called in a plastic surgeon to stitch up his wound and expected a full recovery on all counts. They insisted he stay overnight as a precaution, pumped him full of fluids, and released him the next afternoon to the care of one Abby McBride.

She drove him from one hospital to another, and, as they entered Mannie's room, a Christmas party was forming. Rosa and Seven showed up with a small tree, decorations from the store, and two gallons of André's Christmas eggnog. André and his wife soon followed with an array of desserts so decadent, a rotation of nurses kept dropping in to check on Mannie.

Rosa led everyone in singing Christmas carols and even threatened to climb up on the bedside table to dance until a nurse explained it would never hold her weight.

Carter refused to let go of Abby's hand—or was it she who wouldn't let go of his?

Later, when the room was still, after the laughter had drifted away, the desserts were long gone, and the nurses rested quietly at their stations, "O Holy Night" began to play over the hospital's speakers. Carter glanced down at sleepy Abby and whispered, "This will always be the most incredible and sacred Christmas of my life."

But she would have none of it. "Oh, no, Carter!"

Abby corrected. "Every Christmas is wonderful in its own unique way. Just wait!"

A Santa-sized smile wrapped Carter's face because he absolutely believed her. Like a boy giddy with the anticipation of imagining what could be wrapped in the boxes under the family's lighted tree, Carter could hardly wait to see what the future would bring.

It was then that Abby leaned close, so close her mouth nearly touched Carter's ear. "Merry Christmas, Carter Cross," she breathed, but before he could reply *Merry Christmas* back to her, she twisted his head ever so slightly to press her lips quietly against his.

He would later—when trying to describe the sensation to her—talk about swirling colors of crimson, amber, and gold, except this time the flooding colors stirred delicately together with melodic music, cool breezes, fresh-picked strawberries, and billowing sheets of beckoning silk—oh, and rivers: deep, flowing rivers of warm, dark chocolate.

Chapter 24

The Christmas Choice

Two Months Later

"Here we go!" Abby giggled to Mannie as the old organ drew a breath and began to bellow Mendelssohn's "Wedding March." Abby's eyes seeped sunlight as Mannie gave her hand a proper squeeze.

"Let's do it!" he directed.

And then, in front of a full but hushed audience at the Trinity United Methodist Church in Springfield, Abby pushed Mannie down the aisle so he could give her away in proper fashion to Carter Cross in front of a waiting crowd of family and friends.

Rosa sat beside Lenny, and both profusely wept. Seven and Rick kissed. Yin, the country's newest citizen, cheered. André and Ziva hugged as Carter and Abby cut the most spectacular twelve-layered, white-chocolate wedding cake ever created. Lorella and Joel agreed it was a wedding that bested theirs, since no one needed to run off to the airport in the middle of the party.

❄

A month to the day after the wedding, Mannie McBride quietly passed away at home, with Carter and Abby by his side. Naturally, tears were shed, but it was a day that was surprisingly peaceful. Late in the afternoon, after the funeral home had respectfully taken Mannie's body away, Abby found an envelope on the bedside table that read *Mannie's Obituary.*

"Let it be known that I, Mannie Foster McBride, was blessed with an extraordinary life. I've read Hemingway from the heights of Kilimanjaro. I've studied Pliny from the Colosseum's steps in Rome. I've eaten pupusas in the untamed jungles of El Salvador and Irish stew as I overlooked the Cliffs of Moher. Though I've been brought to tears by the sheer majesty of our world, its grandeur is but a shovelful of soil compared to the mountain of contentment that a tiny and timid three-year-old rag doll of a girl heaped onto my blessed life. She taught me that the miracle isn't in what we accomplish in our lives, but in the relationships we nurture. In place of listing undeserved accolades, let us simply remember to: *LaughMore,* for laughter is the window through which we glimpse the joy of God; *HopeMore,* because tomorrow life will give us another chance; *GiveMore,* for when we share our time, we share our most prized possession; *ForgiveMore,* because as we forgive others, we learn to also forgive ourselves; and *LoveMore,* for while faith may have the power to move mountains, love has the remarkable power to change the human heart."

❄

Eighteen Months Later

The ReadMore Café had never looked more festive, especially on the first Monday in October—but Carter insisted they get a head start on the holiday season.

Abby crafted her trademark display of Christmas books, though it was not an easy job for a woman with a protruding pregnant belly that kept knocking things over. This year, an exciting new addition completed the tree: a book just published by a small New England Press. It was a story that Carter had hoped to call *The Christmas*

Carol, Angel, Box, Wish—because all the best nouns are taken, but the publisher considered the name ridiculous and changed it to *Christmas by Accident*.

It didn't matter. It was a story authored by Carter and Abby Cross about a man who had loved Christmas as a little boy, but as he grew older forgot its meaning for a time, distracted by the cynicism of the world. He remembered the magic of the season when an accident nearly snatched everything away.

As Carter helped Abby straighten the display, a customer entered, spied the Christmas books already out, and rolled his eyes into a scowl.

"Isn't it a bit early?" the grumpy man said to Carter, letting his disgust shower across the room.

Carter's lips turned up. It was his favorite question. "I used to think so," he told the man, "until I met my wife—literally by *accident*—except that's when I learned there are no accidents, only miracles, especially at Christmas. Let me buy you a piece of the most decadent double-chocolate dessert you'll ever taste, and I'll tell you all about it."

Acknowledgments

I've been blessed with funny children. They have, in turn, married witty spouses. It only made sense when I needed humor for this story to rely on their wit and wisdom, for which I am sincerely grateful. I love you all.

Recipes
from the
ReadMore
Café

André's Cinnamon Egglessnog

1 package (3.4 oz.) instant
   French vanilla pudding mix

2 tablespoons sugar

½ teaspoon nutmeg

½ teaspoon cinnamon

⅛ teaspoon ginger

⅛ teaspoon allspice

5 cups milk (whole or 2%)

¾ cup heavy cream

4 tablespoons pure maple syrup

½ teaspoon vanilla extract

¼ teaspoon rum extract (optional)

Combine dry pudding mix, sugar, nutmeg, cinnamon, ginger, and allspice; mix together well.

Combine milk, cream, maple syrup, vanilla, and rum extract in a large bowl. Slowly hand whisk dry ingredients into wet ingredients until mixed thoroughly. (Do not use a blender.)

Refrigerate for at least one hour to thicken (two or three hours is better). Stir well. (If the consistency is thicker than desired, add ½ to 1 cup milk to thin.)

Pour into cups, garnish each with a spoonful of cinnamon whipped cream (next page), sprinkle with freshly ground nutmeg, and enjoy!

Cinnamon Whipped Cream

4 tablespoons powdered sugar
1 teaspoon cinnamon
½ teaspoon nutmeg
1 cup cream

In a small bowl, mix together powdered sugar, cinnamon, and nutmeg.

In a separate bowl, whip cream with beaters or hand whisk while slowly adding dry ingredients. Whip until soft peaks form. (Don't over whip.)

Makes 6 to 8 servings.

Mini Peppermint Chocolate Cheesecakes

Before you begin baking, be sure all the ingredients are at room temperature. They will mix more easily and the finished cheesecakes will have a smoother texture.

Crust:
Purchase a package of your favorite chocolate wafer cookies. *(For a gluten-free option, omit the crust, letting the bottom chocolate cheesecake layer become the crust.)*

Cheesecake Filling:
3 packages (8 ounces each) cream cheese, softened
1 cup sugar
2 tablespoons cornstarch
3 large eggs
½ cup sour cream
1 teaspoon vanilla extract

For Chocolate Filling:
1½ cups semisweet chocolate chips, melted and cooled

For Peppermint Filling:
1 cup crushed peppermint candy canes
(approximately 6 large candy canes)
1 teaspoon peppermint extract

Sour Cream Topping:
1¼ cups sour cream
⅓ cup sugar
1 teaspoon vanilla extract

Garnish:

Chopped peppermint candies and chocolate chunks.

Heat oven to 325 degrees F. Put paper liners in 24 muffin cups. Put a chocolate wafer cookie in each muffin cup.

Filling: Beat cream cheese, sugar, and cornstarch in a large bowl until smooth. Beat in eggs one at a time, just until blended. Fold in sour cream and vanilla. Divide batter between two bowls. Mix melted chocolate into one bowl. Stir crushed peppermint candies and extract into the other bowl of batter.

Put a spoonful of chocolate filling into the bottom of each muffin cup over crust. Carefully smooth until even with a small knife. Spoon peppermint filling over chocolate layer to cover until the cups are almost full. Smooth with knife as before.

Bake 18–20 minutes, being careful to not overbake. Centers should still look soft. They set up as they cool. Cool to room temperature and then refrigerate uncovered several hours to overnight.

Mix ingredients together by hand for sour cream topping. Remove cheesecakes from liners and arrange on serving tray. Spoon sour cream topping over each cheesecake and smooth with back of spoon.

Garnish with chopped chocolate and peppermint pieces. Refrigerate until set, at least one hour.

Makes 24.

Hot and Creamy Christmas Caramel Cocoa

2 cups milk (whole milk preferred)

1 cup heavy cream

5 ounces quality dark chocolate, chopped
(approximately 72% cocoa)

2 tablespoons light brown sugar

1 teaspoon cinnamon

1 teaspoon vanilla extract

¾ cup quality caramel sauce, divided
(Torani brand, if available)

4–5 gingersnap cookies, crushed

Whipped cream

Mix milk and heavy cream in a medium saucepan and heat on medium-low, stirring occasionally, until just before the mixture simmers (the edges will barely begin to bubble). Use a large enough saucepan to ensure it isn't more than half full.

Add chopped chocolate and whisk until melted. Whisk in brown sugar, cinnamon, vanilla, and 1/2 cup of the caramel sauce. Continue to heat for two or three minutes, whisking occasionally. It will thicken slightly. (If it begins to boil, turn down the heat.)

Ladle hot cocoa into mugs until they are half to three-quarters full. Top with whipped cream and sprinkle generously with gingersnap crumbles. Drizzle with remaining caramel sauce. Enjoy!